VOODOO YOU LOVE

A MALVEAUX CURSE MYSTERY (BOOK 4)

G.A. CHASE

BAYOU MOON PRESS, LLC

Bayou Moon Press, LLC

ABOUT THIS BOOK

Kendell Summer thought she was done dealing with the devil, but he's found a way to invade her nightmares— literally. With her soul intimately connected to Colin Malveaux, she can no longer ignore her visions.

Her ruthless adversary now resides in his own private hell, thanks to the dead swamp witch's granddaughter, Sanguine Delarosa. However, Colin, not daunted by imprisonment, has taken control of his demonic realm. Now he wants to use what he's learned to wreak havoc in the land of the living.

Kendell and Sanguine share responsibility for Colin's interdimensional prison. To repair the damage to the walls of hell, the women—together with Myles, the band members, and their canine companions—will need to take a trip to hell and confront the devil himself.

1

olin Malveaux leaned back in his ergonomic office chair—his immobilized broken leg on the desk—and watched the post-hurricane-driven rain batter the French Quarter. It was 6:52 p.m. on Friday, July 18. He didn't need to look at his watch. As near as he could estimate, it had been 6:52 p.m. on Friday, July 18, for the last ten hours. The rain never let up. The sky never changed from dusk to night. His hunger never progressed to starvation, and he feared the fast-food hamburger he'd had for lunch would forever be giving him heartburn. At least he was spared the daily ritual of having to sleep. Now that time had no meaning, he no longer had to endure that irritating waste of time. He found that funny.

He bolted out of his chair and yelled at the storm, "Fuck you, witch! Show yourself!"

Colin didn't really expect an answer. He'd been condemned to her version of hell, and clearly, she was

1

content to sit in hiding and watch her life's accomplishment play out.

"It's not her—it's me." With no one to talk to, he'd resorted to doing his thinking out loud. He would have liked to hear someone telling him that talking to himself was a sign of insanity. "Rain be damned. I need to see if there's anyone else out there. Even in a hurricane, people frequent the Quarter's bars. It's as good a place as any to start. I've been a fool not to make a countermove."

The splint he'd fashioned from the parts of an umbrella was an improvement over the sticks he'd found in the swamp, but walking was still slow going. His broken rib felt like a red-hot iron jabbing into his side. With time at a standstill, he wondered if his injuries from diving headfirst into the hurricane would ever heal.

"The pain does not matter. I'm immortal." He'd spent the hours at his desk considering his strengths and recording them in the dog-eared notebook he'd carried with him since high school. Without a functioning computer, it was the best he could do. Before heading out, he looked over the list one last time to remind himself of what the witch was up against.

- If this is hell and time isn't moving, I can't die. This is a theory that needs to be tested. Worst case, I end up leaving this hell. Best case, I am a god.
- If it turns out that I truly am immortal, I have nothing to lose. The witch will have created an adversary she can't defeat.

- I need to find Baron Samedi's cane. It must be here somewhere. Once I have that, I can cross from here to Guinee or perhaps even return to life.
- Hell must have guardians. The old swamp witch must be here somewhere—as must Baron Samedi. I need to face my adversaries.

He stared back out the window, searching for any sign of life. "Am I really the only person in this hell?" That was the question and not one he'd be able to answer while sitting in his office.

Colin couldn't see a single light in a single window from his office, but the witch had seen fit to leave his high-rise partially functional and the elevator that took him to his office penthouse in full working order. He assumed that was meant to taunt him, since only from the highest perch in New Orleans could he truly see how deserted the city was. "What good is it to be a god without anyone to rule over?"

The question wasn't just rhetorical. In asking it, he'd stumbled on what he believed to be the witch's true mistake. She'd created a god then underestimated his desire for followers.

He saw no point in protecting himself from the wind and rain. Post-hurricane winds seldom obeyed the laws of gravity. An umbrella would have to cover him down to the toes of his badly scuffed dress shoes to prevent him from getting soaked.

Though he'd already confirmed there were no cars in

this witch's dungeon, a lifetime of conditioning had him checking the road anyway. "Stupid. I need to not just learn the laws of this reality but accept them as well. Rule one: I can't be killed."

Colin dragged his leg across Canal Street, feeling grateful not to have to dodge traffic and tourists. On the other side, he fell against the nearest shop. In another reality, it had been a tacky, brightly colored tourist trap selling gaudy beads, T-shirts, and plastic masks. He rubbed a clear spot on the glass and looked into the retail space. Not only was there no merchandise, but there were no displays, or anything else for that matter—just bare plaster-and-brick walls and an empty concrete floor. Either the owners had somehow managed to squirrel away every stick of furniture, the looters had started early and been remarkably thorough, or this reality didn't care much for tourism. If that last option were the case, he'd finally found some commonality with the old swamp witch. "Good riddance."

Poppies Chicken, unfortunately, was also nothing more than a sorrowful empty space. For a moment, he considered breaking in to see if the witch had unintentionally left some product in the freezer. He'd never worked in fast food—or any other service job for that matter. "How hard could it be to fry up some chicken?" The effort didn't seem worth the reward. He already had enough fast-food heartburn.

Each window he looked in told the same story. This French Quarter was only a façade. Like some Hollywood South soundstage that hadn't bothered with anything beyond what the camera would capture, this reality was a mockery of the real thing. The lack of broken windows and graffiti confirmed that even the city's delinquents had escaped the witch's hell. "You know, to have really tortured me, you should have spray-painted some gang signs— something to make it look like there were still people present, to give me hope, but then make it clear they're thugs I should fear."

He knew she'd see through the ruse. He'd have become the leader of a band of miscreants easily enough. The whole damn scene reminded him of a fish in a bowl with fake plastic ships and castles to swim through.

"But my office is real." The thought made him turn to the towering marble building at the end of the block. New Orleans Bank and Trust had been his mother's domain, but long before her, Baron Malveaux had used the institution to establish the family's wealth and prestige. And now the baron was a part of Colin.

"If the Lincoln Laroque side of me gets to keep the penthouse office, I expect you'll extend the same courtesy to Baron Malveaux."

Water flowed off the grand marble stairs that led up to the imposing structure like an aquatic feature in some ill-conceived, overfunded public-works art project. His clothes were already soaked so completely they clung to every piece of skin they touched.

The stitching on his Ferragamos was fraying badly from the abuse. He took a deep breath and trusted his weight to the smooth sole of the finely made shoe on the slick step. "Still standing. You're going to have to do better than a driving rain to knock me on my ass." He assumed she understood the defiance to be more figurative than literal.

When he reached the top, he saw the door to the bank standing open. He shook his head in disgust. "It doesn't do you any good now. You would have had to make it look like there was someone in this hell with me while I didn't expect it. Unless, of course, you've got my mother in there. Now, that would be a surprise."

He really hoped to confront Baron Samedi on the other side of that door. The voodoo loa of the dead had followed Colin into the hurricane while he chased after the dark spirit's walking cane. "Man, I could really use that thing now, and not just for its metaphysical properties."

The hope that the cane had somehow made the transition from the land of the living to the witch's hell was the one driving force that kept him going. With the cane, he might have the power to confront his captor. If the stick could make it from Guinee to life, Colin saw no reason that it couldn't also exist in hell. He'd followed it into the hurricane. "It must be here somewhere."

But that meant Baron Samedi was likely also in this hell. Two supernatural beings against one greedy businessman might not be the best of odds, but neither of his opponents had his resolve.

Not that time mattered, but physical exertion still had a way of making Colin stop to catch his breath. He guessed it took most of what he would have known as the morning to get to the bank and climb the stairs to the third floor. Hobbling along on the old wood floors renewed his sense of self-importance. This was where he'd established his seventh gate of Guinee—where he'd stood in judgment of all who'd died and wished to continue on to the *deep waters.*

The portraits of the past bank presidents were missing, as was anything else to indicate the bank had once been the center of commerce in the city. "So long as my fucking office is intact."

He stopped at the expanse of bare wall where the elegantly carved mahogany door was supposed to be. "So you started building this hell even before I possessed that idiot of a bartender."

He'd hidden his office's location so artfully that for the hundred and fifty years that Baron Malveaux had been buried in the above-ground crypt, no one had discovered it concealed behind the thin plaster. He ran his hand along the wall and felt the subtle change in texture. It was still there, but simply breaking down the wall wouldn't work. He'd be left with only plaster dust and splintered wood. It would take an object from Guinee, like the magic cane, to break the barrier. "I'll be back."

Colin hadn't expected to find his office at the bank standing wide open. That would have been too easy. If he had access to Guinee, then he'd also find a way back to the living. All he'd needed was to feel the difference in textures. Either the witch had done such an excellent job of re-creating reality that she'd seen to the smallest of details, or the bank was somehow connected to the one remembered.

He sat on the marble staircase and considered the two options out loud. "The rest of the Quarter is all façade. If you'd really wanted to go into so much detail that I could feel the change in wall texture, I'd expect more detail in the other buildings as well."

Then there was his office in the Central Business District high-rise. "Places that I'm connected to are exceptions to the rest of the buildings. Like a movie set, they had to be more detailed due to their usage. That would mean this bank is to be one of the sets in your demented little play. The question is, did you design these sets, or are they interdimensionally connected to my reality?"

He didn't have an answer, but what he did have was time. "If I assume this bank isn't just a reproduction, I'll need an object connected to Guinee to open the seventh gate. I may not have Baron Samedi's cane, and therefore his powers, but I do have friends in that version of the beyond. It's a start anyway."

He struggled to his feet and headed to the door. Baron Malveaux had dealt extensively with Marie Laveau, and Lincoln Laroque had been duped by her descendent Delphine de Galpion. Whatever remained of both women in this carnival funhouse of a reality would be hidden away in Scratch and Sniff Perfumery's back room.

He returned to the tempest outside to continue his exploration. At least the voodoo madam's shop wasn't far. Every building he passed had locked doors, but the old wooden shack in the residential section of the Quarter had been so termite eaten and weather damaged that modern deadbolts were useless. And without Delphine de Galpion in this realm, there wouldn't be any of her handy little curses to deny him entry. The wooden steps squished under his shoes.

The part of him that had been frightened and intrigued about meeting the mystical woman so many years ago argued he should at least knock. In defiance of his foolishness, he put his shoulder to the door with all of his weight. The ensuing burst of pain from his ribs made him lose his breath.

"Damn you to hell." He directed his irritation and anger at the old swamp witch and would continue to do so until he escaped.

If he had two good legs, he'd have kicked the door in. In his current condition, he decided to try the doorknob instead. "Locked? Really?"

This wasn't his domain. Though much of his history had been collected in the back room of the building, he'd never been welcomed with open arms by the voodoo priestess. With all of the windows shuttered, he couldn't be sure if the priestess's shack was more of the witch's fakery or a prospect worth pursuing.

"What do I have to lose?"

The finesse required to pick a skeleton key lock had never been his strong suit, but he was unable to simply force the door open. "When I get back to the living, first thing I'm doing is buying a hardware store. What I wouldn't give for a good pry bar right now."

He hobbled back to the street in search of anything he could use against the unyielding door. "Those fucking termites must all be holding hands. Somewhere out here, there has to be a house with less determined bugs. I just need something to use for bashing that door in."

He struggled away from the Quarter in his search. Each

house he passed had either been remodeled—usually with money supplied from his family's bank—or securely boarded up. He reached for the fence railing in front of the next shotgun double to help him along. The wrought-iron bar shook so badly he nearly missed his step. "Perfect."

He pushed and pulled at the rust-weakened bar until it finally came free of its fellow soldiers. It wasn't the Samedi cane, but the iron rod made him feel invincible. Eyeing the rest of the rails, he knew they too might come in handy. "I've been reduced to Iron Age tools. One problem at a time."

He turned back to the shop and dragged the bar along the concrete curb to sharpen the end. When he got back to Delphine's shop, he didn't bother with the stairs. From the sidewalk, he thrust the iron bar into the doorknob with such ferocity that it sailed halfway through the door. The weathered wood looked as though it had been harpooned. He refrained from expressing his feeling of satisfaction. There was still too far to go before he could claim any victory.

The door opened with only a slight push. He pulled the bar out like a warrior who'd just skewered his adversary with a sword. The front room, where Delphine kept the fragrances she used for mixing her potions, was empty— just like every other building in the Quarter.

"Don't get discouraged. The bank's lobby was empty too."

As he approached the curtain to the back room, he began to understand why people prayed. It had nothing to do with believing a greater being would heed their request and everything to do with thinking they could change reality through force of will.

He ripped the curtain halfway off of the rod. "Since I seem to be alone in this world, I decree that no room will remain closed to my desires."

His heart beat faster at seeing that her office retained the curio cabinets filled with voodoo fetishes. He squeezed around the largest wood-and-glass unit and into the room hidden behind it. He'd never been so happy to see Delphine's gaudy African-motif throne. He fell into the chair and looked around at her walls of journals and artifacts with a renewed sense of optimism.

2

"We should move in together." Kendell's words ricocheted around in Myles's brain like a bullet fired into a steel drum.

Not that the idea hadn't been hinted at. After nearly a year of dating, they'd managed to avoid the inevitable for longer than he thought possible. Still, some ideas had to be approached with all the skill of a bomb-disposal unit.

"I thought you liked your independence."

Her laugh didn't help. "You should see your face. I'm not talking about getting *married*."

From her emphasis on the word, he could tell she'd intentionally tried to make him squirm. "So you don't want to move in together?"

Her blush often said more than her words. "I love you, and I know you feel the same about me. But my proposal is *not* based on our relationship. It isn't even a matter of saving money or some bullshit like that. We've been through a couple of life-threatening—and soul-stealing—adventures. I feel safer when you're around. And without trying to infringe on your masculinity, I worry about you on the nights that you're not here."

From the bed, he looked around her girly bedroom, wondering how he'd fit in. "I suppose with Colin in hell, we'll have to be watching our backs. Sanguine's explanation of her grandmother's metaphysical cage didn't exactly inspire confidence."

She rolled her cup of morning coffee between her hands as she sat next to him in her oversized nightshirt. "It's not like we won't have our own lives. With me working mornings at the coffee shop and you working nights at the bar, we're already finding it hard to spend time together."

"And the nights that I am off, you're usually playing with the band. I suppose being threatened by evil spirits is one of the few things we end up doing together. We should look into changing that."

Her big smoky-brown eyes had a way of melting his resolve. "Living together could make that easier. I wouldn't suggest we live here. We could find a place that would work for both of us."

"I suppose you've already talked this over with Cheesecake?"

The Lhasa apso hurried into the room at hearing her name. "She would have let you move in from the day you rescued her from the dognappers. A girl doesn't forget that kind of thing—and a human girl doesn't either."

He'd played the delaying tactic too many times, and she had a valid point. If anything, each time they thought they'd won, their adversary grew stronger. "I'd want to stay in the Quarter. I know the Marigny or Bywater might make more sense, and we could get more space for the money, but this feels like where I belong."

"No argument there. I'll start poking around after work. Polly says she has a Realtor who's good at finding reasonably priced rentals. She even has an in for getting a place in the Lower Pontalba."

"Would you really want to live on Jackson Square?" He realized too late that he'd been seduced into agreeing to her proposal.

~

CHARLIE STOOD AT THE BAR, holding a bottle of scotch in one and a glass half-filled with ice in the other. His mouth was open far too dramatically. "Dude. Tell me you're joking."

Myles continued making up the rum and Coke for the early evening customer. "Knock it off. You know we've been dating for nearly a year. It's not like anything's going to change."

The lead bartender returned to his duties. "Keep telling yourself that. Who am I going to party with? All our adventures? I'm disappointed in you."

Myles had allowed his friend to rib him long enough. "You like Kendell."

"No doubt. She's not my type, but that dark, mysteriously witchy vibe is undeniable. My opposition has nothing to do with her personally." He grabbed a bottle of El

Dorado 12 Year Old rum. "I will bet you this bottle that *things change* by this time next year."

Myles was beginning to get testy. "I'm not going anywhere. Kendell's not going to quit singing. We both love our independence. So knock it off."

Charlie turned to the guitarist who led the house band. "Hey, Jackson, what's that Beatles song about a guy who's married to a singer?"

The guy started strumming "Ob-La-Di, Ob-La-Da." The few regulars in the bar quickly picked up on the joke and substituted Myles for Desmond and Kendell for Molly in the lyrics. Everyone sang along, much to Myles's humiliation—especially when he was the one putting on his pretty face to become a singer with the band.

"Very funny."

Charlie could be an ass, but he knew when he'd taken a joke far enough. "Just don't go getting another dog. That's always the next step. Cheesecake will forever be Kendell's mutt, but if you guys get another pooch, it'll be more binding than a wedding ring."

"What would I do with a dog? Kendell would be the first to tell you I can barely look after myself. No way she'd trust me with another living being."

"Well, that's the truth. You only get by..." Charlie pointed at the guitarist, who broke into, "With a Little Help from My Friends."

This is going to be a long night.

~

KENDELL NEVER REALIZED there were so many hidden bungalows, old slave quarters, and lofts available for rent in the seventy-eight square blocks of the French Quarter. "Thanks for coming with me. I'm afraid I really don't know much about apartment hunting. I lucked into the place on Decatur Street."

When it was just the two of them, Polly liked to walk arm in arm with Kendell. Every man, and most women, took quick glances at the couple as they sauntered down the street.

"Are you kidding?" Polly said. "I haven't seen the inside of the Lower Pontalba since I had that one-night stand, and I wasn't spending a lot of time admiring the architecture, if you know what I mean."

"I'll bet you got a good look at the crown moldings."

Polly hip-checked Kendell for the comment. "All I meant was it's not the kind of place girls like us usually find for rent. *Snazzy* would be the term I'd use. At least that's what the Louisiana State Museum, which manages the building, is hoping for."

As they walked past Saint Louis Cathedral, Kendell admired the four-story Lower Pontalba that took up the entire next block. "You know Myles and I can't afford this."

"No one can. At least not anyone who works for a living. But since you *are* looking for a place and I *do* have a friend who's a Realtor, what's the harm in doing a little window shopping?"

Though she knew what Polly meant, the mention of windows made Kendell inspect the elegant verandas. "Still with the double-hung windows? For these prices, you'd think they'd upgrade to French doors."

"Keeps you limber. Plus, they're better at keeping the rain out during a storm."

As Polly's Realtor ushered them into the grand apartment, Kendell knew looking at it would be waste of time even if she had the money. "I don't know. Seems awfully upscale. Cheesecake's not a big fan of snooty people for neighbors. She likes her comfort. And Myles would never fit in."

Polly, however, intended to enjoy the opulence. "Just look at all this light. They must have remodeled within the last year. Everything's so new and clean." She twirled around the living room, which was full of historically correct details. "Living here would be like being a Disney princess."

"Okay, Cinderella, but I've got to find someplace reasonable. I can't show Myles this. He's barely hanging onto the string of moving in together."

Polly sighed and gave a cheek kiss to her Realtor. "A girl can try. Thanks for taking the time to let us see it."

"No problem. It gives me a chance to daydream too."

Back out on the street, Polly was less excited about the next prospect. "Why are you two moving in together anyway? I thought you liked living on your own."

"I do. That's why we need a place big enough so we won't be under each other's feet all the time. Do you think I'm making a mistake?"

Polly could be pretty harsh on people she was still evaluating, but once she'd made up her mind, she was a die-hard friend. "I told you before, Myles is one of the good ones. Doesn't mean I'm going to quit ribbing him, but between you and me, he's definitely long-term-relationship material. I'm just wondering if this is you wanting a live-in boyfriend or a bodyguard."

Kendell watched the broken, uneven concrete as she walked. "You're not wrong. But it's not just about him riding to my rescue like some white knight. I've saved him too, thanks in part to you and the band. I could deal with the dangerous world. It's the dangerous beyond that makes me want to hold him and Cheesecake tight."

Polly had been there when they'd released the power of Baron Samedi's cane. She'd helped free Myles from the baron Malveaux. She'd even rounded up the band to help rescue Cheesecake in Float World from her abductors. Few knew of the dangers Kendell faced. Fewer had stood shoulder to shoulder with her through every battle.

"I'm not judging," Polly said. "I just want to be sure you know what you're getting into. Guys have a way of seeing living together as leading to something more permanent."

Though Kendell had joked with Myles about marriage, such an idea wasn't even on the horizon. "If I've learned anything from my study of voodoo and my time traveling the nether worlds with Myles, it's to live in the moment." She looked up at a faded sign that hung from a third-floor balcony. "And at this moment, I'd like to check out that apartment."

Having spent the day looking at apartments—from recently remodeled, overpriced ones to run-down hovels that she wouldn't feel comfortable letting Cheesecake take a piss in—she'd begun to despair. Polly had been a great companion. Her optimism and excitement made the project feel like shopping at high-end clothing stores with a dear friend, but they weren't just browsing. Kendell needed to have something to show to Myles, and she didn't have much time left in the day.

They passed the small bakery that occupied the ground floor and opened the green door to the alleyway that led to the back of the building. As they closed the door to the street, Polly whispered, "Every time I sneak into one of these hidden passageways, I feel like I'm going back in time."

"I usually feel like someone's going to jump me. At least this one has electric lights instead of those damn gaslights. Those things never put out enough light." The grand archway at the back of the building opened up to a courtyard garden with three-story-tall brick walls on all sides. Kendell stared up at the open balconies. "This is nice and private."

"Yeah. Perfect place for Myles to contact his loa-of-the-dead friends. I think *creepy* was the word you were looking for."

Kendell brushed off Polly's hesitation. The place had an old-world charm that hadn't been glossed over by a modern contractor with more desire for money than authenticity. Fortunately, the stairs that led up to the small balcony connecting the apartments had been rebuilt. The balcony overlooked a small oasis.

"Cross your fingers," Kendell said. "I'd like to finish this adventure before it starts getting dark."

Two adjoining doors led into the apartment. Polly pushed open the kitchen door. "First impression?"

It had become a standard question. So far, the places that didn't survive Kendell's first glance hadn't recovered, no matter what amenities they had. "Light, airy, not overly ostentatious but certainly not a man cave. So far, so good." She ran her hand along the brick wall. At one time, the whole place had been plastered over, but interior decorators had found that cutting the plaster to look as though it had fallen off the walls made for nice patterns of smooth white finish and rough red brick. When an apartment was in a state of decay, the result was depressing and eerie. As a fashion statement, though, the effect was quite compelling.

Polly was much better than Kendell at breaking down strengths and weaknesses, both in people and in places. "Decent stainless-steel appliances—not new, so you won't get dinged for damaging the finish, but functional. I do like the light fixtures."

"The kitchen's not very large, but then, neither of us likes to cook."

The place had the traditional confusing layout of old apartments that had been initially designed as a single palatial family residence. Kendell had to catch her breath when she opened the door to the living room with its three sets of French doors. Each one led out to a terrace lit by the early evening. "Sold."

Polly laughed. "Don't you think Myles should have a look before you plop down his bar tips?"

Kendell was only barely paying attention. "Look at all

that lovely cast-iron latticework. It's even nicer than my place on Decatur."

"And bigger." Polly opened the restored glass doors to the large balcony. "And you'd have the whole space—no more sharing with your neighbors."

Kendell tried to remain analytical, but all she could come up with were the apartment's selling points. "The location is perfect. The space is amazing. Everything's so much newer than in either of our apartments."

"I wouldn't include Myles's place for your comparisons. A doghouse would have more amenities. Didn't anyone tell him slave quarters are supposed to be remodeled into something modern before they're rented out?"

Kendell didn't mind Polly's jabs, especially when Myles wasn't around to take offense. "His place isn't that bad, but I agree—anything I find is bound to be better."

"So I guess the real question is, how will Cheesecake feel?"

MYLES REMEMBERED something he'd heard on a touristy carriage ride through the Quarter about each Creole wedding couple being locked in their apartment until they'd consummated their relationship. He only had a handful of items that Kendell deemed acceptable, but everyone was helping him move them—and nearly everything she owned —to the new place. He felt distinctly as though he was being set up.

But he had to admit the place was pretty amazing. "At

least being on the third floor, I won't have to worry about what I'm wearing when I sneak out to the terrace at night. Though I guess I'm going to have to hit up Papa Ghede about paying me for my services."

Kendell hugged him tightly. He wasn't sure he'd ever seen her so happy when it didn't involve Cheesecake—either the dog or the dessert. "We'll get by. It's not like either of us spends much money. I'm just happy you agreed to move in together. I'm starting to feel like a real grown-up."

"Life isn't too bad now that we're not being hounded by the dead." He knew the break was temporary, but that made the time to explore his relationship with Kendell all the more precious.

Cheesecake ran from room to room then out through one door to the balcony and back in through another. She looked like she was trying every access to make sure they all worked.

Charlie served up drinks to keep everyone in the right frame of mind. Kendell's bandmates from Polly Urethane and the Strippers arranged the furnishings—then rearranged them. The women worked like a design committee that didn't seek his input. By the end of the day, everyone was crashed in the eclectically decorated living room.

Myles lounged back against the arm of the newly acquired used-furniture-store couch with Kendell snuggled tightly to his side. "You guys did a remarkable job. In less than eight hours, I went from living in my *man dungeon*—as Kendell called it—to third-floor luxury."

Charlie passed him a rum and Coke. "Just don't expect

me to move you every weekend. Hanging around with you is giving me a workout."

"I know we've been leaning on everyone here quite a lot lately," Myles said. "You guys are all more than friends. It'd be too easy to call you family. Even family wouldn't put up with what we've put you through."

Polly got up from one of the floor cushions. "When Myles starts getting sappy, I know it's time to go. It's that damn rum—it makes you all sentimental. You're a lot more fun when you drink beer."

Kendell tossed a pillow at her. "Just because you're a coldhearted bitch."

"And tequila, my dear Olympia Stain, makes you feisty. Band practice is tomorrow afternoon, so don't spend all night fooling around in your new love nest." Kendell always smiled when Polly referred to her by her stage name.

Myles felt the effects of the alcohol as he stood up. Polly was probably right about him being a little emotional, but nothing he felt was untrue. He gave each of their friends a big hug before they headed out.

Left with only Kendell and Cheesecake, he finally explored every room of the apartment. "I think we're going to be happy here."

She said, "I'm always happy with you," but she looked concerned.

"What is it?"

"We haven't heard from Papa Ghede lately. And I've been having nightmares I have trouble figuring out. In my dreams, I'm here in the Quarter, but everyone's gone, and it's not really me."

Myles grabbed the mostly empty bottle of rum and took her out to the terrace. "Both Delphine and Sanguine said you're connected to Colin Malveaux through the curse. With him in hell, do you think you're reading some of this thoughts?"

"I think I need to talk to both of them. There must be some way to isolate my mind from him. Sanguine said her grandmother designed her version of hell to cut Colin off from every person. So why can *I* hear him? I'm worried there's something wrong with me—or worse, her cage isn't holding up."

He knew they'd both been slacking on their duties to the afterlife. "I suppose waiting around for Baron Samedi to free himself hasn't been the most productive of plans. The last thing I need is a pissed-off loa of the dead."

He located the shot glass that he reserved for contacting the voodoo loa. Then he set it on the table and filled it from the bottle of rum. A dark man in a dusty long coat and top hat materialized, looking more ragged than Myles remembered.

"Are you ready to get back to work?" the man asked.

Myles considered giving him a sarcastic response. After all, it wasn't as if the guardians of the dead were paying him to be their living lackey. But the spirit looked so drained that Myles knew things weren't going well in Guinee. "What are we up against?"

Papa Ghede drank his rum but didn't refill the glass— definitely a bad sign. "Without Baron Samedi at my side, Baron Kriminel has been gathering followers. I think he intends to take over Guinee."

Kendell nearly dropped her glass. "But you're the supreme loa. You're the first. I didn't think Guinee was susceptible to political bullshit."

"You've just stumbled on the problem with giving other entities freewill, be they humans or gods. Eventually, someone always thinks they can do a better job. Though Guinee isn't your problem, freeing Baron Samedi is. Since he isn't in Guinee—and you haven't heard from him among the living—I have to believe he's stuck in your Wiccan witch's hell."

A cold breeze from the river sent a chill down Myles's back. "How exactly do you propose we rescue him?"

"You'll have to go to hell, but based on your belief in the *deep waters* and Kendell's study of voodoo, neither of you has the doctrine needed to cross over."

Kendell nearly bolted from her chair. "No way. I'm not dragging Sanguine into this. She's done all she can to secure Colin from both life and Guinee."

Myles understood her outburst. The young swamp witch had one job—to tempt Colin into her dead grandmother's clutches. She'd performed admirably. "Kendell's right. All Marie Laveau intended was for the Wiccan witches to be guardians of the curse, not active participants."

Papa Ghede toyed with his empty glass but still refrained from refilling it. "Agnes Delarosa took it on herself to build Colin Malveaux's hell. Her granddaughter willingly went along with the plan. Someone must be watching over that portal between the living and hell." He looked up to stare into Kendell's eyes. "Have you noticed any weaknesses in the jail cell? My bet is you have. We all know of Malveaux's determination."

She settled back into her chair. "If we do nothing, he'll come back." She didn't say it as a question but as a truth she hadn't wanted to face.

"With no one else in that hell, he'll learn to rule a realm of the afterlife."

She nodded. "So he'll come back as a god?"

"That's my concern. While he was in Guinee, I had some control over him, but now that he's tasted his own reality, there will be no containing him should he escape. We have to go all in for Agnes's hell. But as of now, that realm may not be strong enough to contain him. Especially if he gets to Baron Samedi before you do."

o the casual observer, Kendell's lunch with Delphine de Galpion and Sanguine Delarosa might have looked like nothing more than three good friends at their weekly get-together. The topic, however, necessitated that their meeting be conducted in the private garden courtyard of a gumbo shop Delphine had recommended. Noticing the animosity that lurked under the layer of civility between Sanguine and Delphine, Kendell thought, *Looks can be deceiving.*

"We shouldn't all be in one place at the same time," Sanguine said.

Her paranoia was all too often justified. Kendell reached over the wrought-iron-and-glass table and took her hand. "Colin is in hell. Who's going to come after us?"

The beautiful young swamp witch wasn't easily pacified. "The Malveaux curse is nothing to be trifled with. You above all people know that. The three of us at this table are all that stands in the way of Colin realizing his full potential."

Delphine had never been shy about expressing her views of Sanguine or her deceased grandmother. "Agnes Delarosa created Colin's hell, and you inherited it. I'm only here to offer you my knowledge. This is all in your hands."

"Fine." Sanguine had the defiant tone she often used when confronted. "But it's your ancestor who created the curse in the first place."

The argument threatened to ruin Kendell's enjoyment of her crawfish étouffée. "I didn't invite you two to lunch just to have you fight. I've been having nightmares." She let the word *nightmares* dangle out there like a fisherman waiting for a bite.

Sanguine uncharacteristically dabbed at her mouth with her napkin. "What kind of nightmares?"

"I think you know, and I think you've been having them too."

Delphine could be a hard-ass, but she also had an ability to read danger signals. "I was afraid something like this would happen. Agnes Delarosa believed a stagnant hell would be enough to hold Colin, but if a rat is left in a cage with nothing else to do, he'll find a way to chew through the bars. You two are the cage that holds him. If you're getting messages from his hell, we have to act. What do you need?"

After the conversation with Papa Ghede, Kendell had thrashed out the possibilities with Myles for most of the night. "I need a way into hell. I'm part of the curse, so I have to go. If there's a weakness in the walls of Colin's realm, it'll have to be patched from the inside. Myles's connection to

Baron Samedi means he's going too—not that he needed a reason. He wasn't about to agree to this without accompanying me. But we can't make the trip alone."

Sanguine took a spoonful of her turtle soup before replying. "You think I can get you there? I have only the most basic idea of what my grandmother created. I tossed Samedi's walking stick into my grandmother's hurricane, and Colin dove in after it. After she got what she wanted, the door slammed shut."

Delphine pushed her shrimp rémoulade salad aside. "So that's why you need me. The way into the Wiccan hell isn't through the witch's knowledge. You're expecting a voodoo back door."

Myles was right. There is a back entrance. Fuck. "It's going to have to be a good-sized passage. Myles has taken me and Cheesecake on his psychometric journeys before. He even took you with us once. But I'm not sure his soul can handle bringing Baron Samedi back along with me and Sanguine."

"Wait a minute, sister," Sanguine said. "I never said anything about visiting my grandmother's hell."

Kendell hated pressuring Sanguine, but her assistance was vital to their success. "Neither Myles nor I know the first thing about Wicca. Without you there, we'll be trapped. Colin will have all the power, and we'll be at his mercy."

She could tell the young swamp witch really wanted to let loose with some choice expletives. It was a testament to their bond that she refrained. "You're going to owe me an ice cream when this is over."

Kendell laughed at the childlike response from the woman who was not much younger than she was. "I already owe you a lot more than that. Any thoughts on how we enter your grandmother's version of Guinee?"

Sanguine quickly reverted to her irritating self-righteousness. "You people and your mystical realms. I'll bet Cheesecake was some kind of unicorn in that fanciful world. Agnes's hell isn't like Guinee. It's a real place—or rather, dimension." Sanguine waved her hand at the sky. "Guinee is like some fictitious place."

If it were anyone else, Kendell would have been preparing for battle, but Sanguine had proved herself to be correct too many times for Kendell to argue with her. "Cheesecake would like you to know she was a very large wolf, thank you very much. Guinee isn't some world made up by little girls playing in their rooms."

"I didn't mean to disparage your religion. All I meant was, if we go on some spiritual journey to get there, we'll be no more than ghosts. I'm not sure that would do us much good. Scaring someone already condemned to hell doesn't seem useful. Besides, his realm isn't connected to the *deep waters*."

Kendell began to understand. "So that's what makes it hell? Colin can't ever connect to humanity because he's denied that basic human right?"

Sanguine took a sip of her iced sweet tea. "That's how Agnes secured him from dumping his greed back into every person."

Kendell wondered if such a fate was justified. "But that's only while he's in hell, right? What happens when he dies?"

"So long as he's alive, the longer he's in that realm, the thinner the bond to people will become. It's like a rope that's slowly fraying but is never completely severed. Even I don't know what happens once he dies. Agnes could only build her hell from the land of the living. Now that she's passed on, I would guess she's got something special prepared for him when they meet again."

Kendell turned back to the voodoo priestess. "Any thoughts on how we convert Myles's abilities into a gate to hell?"

"It's not that easy. You physically will have to leave this dimension—just like Colin did. But as Sanguine said, we can't exactly call forth Agnes as a hurricane. You need something from this reality that connects to something in that hell."

"What about the cursed items from Baron Malveaux that Colin wears? Those were the things that let me keep track of him while he was chasing Sanguine through the swamp."

Delphine shook her head. "Not good enough, not this time. It has to be something that's actually mated to something in hell. If you had one of his cufflinks and he had the other, that might work, but he showed me that he was wearing them both."

"We do have something," Sanguine said. "And it's so obvious. The silver skull we pulled off Baron Samedi's cane. Nothing would be more connected than that. Assuming, of course, that the cane ended up in Agnes's hell."

A plan began to form for Kendell. "We didn't find the staff among the living, and Papa Ghede is positive it's not in Guinee. Where else could it be?"

Delphine wasn't finished. "That's just the first step. You're talking about multiple people crossing over. That's going to take a lot more than just putting your hands on the skull like some kind of magical transportation object. You'll need to infuse it with energy like what Agnes did with her little hurricane."

Kendell knew right where she'd hidden the skull. "It's not very powerful, but it would seat plenty of people."

"What are you talking about?" Delphine asked.

"I gave the skull to Minerva to hide with Fleurentine Malveaux's other possessions. Minerva thought it would make a nice gearshift knob for her VW bus."

"Crude, but it could work. The energy needed is less about force than emotion. And I may be able to whip up a little turbo-spell to move that old van along a little faster."

~

MINERVA WAX LEANED against her vintage VW with her arms crossed, like a mother deciding whether Kendell was good enough to take her child on a date. The remaining three members of the band gathered around her.

"Do you or Myles even know how to drive a stick shift?" Minerva asked.

"I drive my little scooter around town. How different can it be?"

The drummer dropped her arms to her sides. "That settles it. I'm coming with you."

Polly stepped next to Minerva. "We all are. It's not like we can play a gig without our lead guitarist."

Kendell loved her band for always wanting to stand together, but some destinations were only for the most foolhardy. "We're going to *hell*. This is not some gig in Kenner. I'm talking actual hell here."

"All the more reason," Minerva said. "I've always joked that this old bus has taken me to hell and back. Time for my old girl to make an honest woman of me."

The bus looked the part. When Minerva inherited it from her grandfather, it had been decked out as a hippie wagon, but the whole band had pitched in to paint it with images of Dia de los Muertos sugar skulls on a black background. The interior had never lost the early '70s upholstery of brightly colored Mexican blankets and dayglow stickers.

"This is stupid," Kendell said. "You can't go. I won't let you. End of story. I just need your bus. It's a lot to ask, I know. But you're all aware of the consequences if I ignore the warnings."

Minerva dangled the keys off her finger. "Sorry, me and my bus come as a matched set."

"Just like the whole band," Polly said.

Lynn Seed had a tendency to find the logical argument when everyone else chose emotion, and vice versa. "Think about it, Kendell. You're going to have to use magic in hell. We all know your power lies in your music. Now, you could play on your little guitar, and I'm sure that would impress the hell out of the devil, but your music is stronger with us backing you up."

"We're all badass women," Scraper said. "What's more badass than playing a gig in hell? Count me in."

Kendell turned to Myles. "Would you please say something?"

"If it were up to me, I'd go alone. But you'd never stand for that. Just like your girls won't stand for being left out. I can't think of a single time they haven't shown up to a rescue. I don't like the idea of risking anyone, but your girls have proven to be pretty handy in a fight."

"Next you're going to tell me I should bring Cheesecake."

Myles shrugged. "She's been a she-wolf before."

∽

WITH KENDELL at work at the coffee shop, Myles considered his next move. Getting out of his old place hadn't just been about satisfying her needs. So long as he didn't register a change of address, the police would be left guessing about his location, but it wouldn't take them long to piece together that he'd moved in with his girlfriend.

The scene of the cop cars camped out in front of his apartment as he was on the run in the stolen van with Joe Cazenave—one-time lieutenant in the force—and Professor Yates continued to haunt him. It could have been nothing, but with Chief of Police Gerald Laroque trying to distance himself from any paranormal investigation into his extended family, Myles had to believe he would at least be forced to spend a night in jail. If Chief Laroque needed a scapegoat to keep his family quiet, Myles feared he was the most likely choice.

Joe was the problem. The last thing he'd said was that if he was back on the force, Myles would know everything had returned to normal. But how was Myles to find out? Walking into the huge marble police station seemed like a good way to inadvertently turn himself in. He needed every ally he could find among the living, and no one had more connections than Joe Cazenave.

Out on the veranda, Myles turned away from the police station to look out toward the Mississippi River. He had one other ally to check in on, and though the professor might not be as useful as Joe, contacting him didn't involve the risk of incarceration. *No use putting it off any longer.*

As he headed out of the building, he grabbed his beat-up bicycle from under the stairs. It wasn't a long distance to the wharf, but with the ever-present police, he didn't want to rely on his Sketchers for mobility.

The bike chain squealed as he got up to speed and headed away from the river toward Rampart Street. One block up, he turned onto a quiet residential street. Zigzagging his way through the Quarter, he made his way to Esplanade Avenue. The large-limbed oak trees that occupied the garden-like division of the main thoroughfare nicely shaded the bike path. Gutter punks had found the area pleasant enough to use for their daytime siestas. Any cop who might be in the area found himself busy with paranoid tourists who thought the miscreant sleeping youths were out to get them. The distraction gave Myles peace of mind. He'd be the last person someone would be complaining about.

Professor Yates's laboratory hadn't improved since Myles's last visit. The carnival-like gypsy trailer he used for his steampunk-mystic fortuneteller con was parked on the dock. Other than that, the old shipping office looked to be abandoned.

Myles knocked on the boarded-up glass door. "Professor, are you home?"

The sound of equipment falling over preceded the old man's call for Myles to come in.

"Would you look at what they did to my instruments? For an organization devoted to keeping mystical objects safely out of the hands of the general public, Luther Noire's little operation doesn't know the first thing about how to handle scientific gear."

Myles wasn't convinced the mayhem that covered every metal desk left over from the shipping company was anyone's fault but the professor's. "They just dumped this stuff here?"

"Oh, hell no. You think I'd let those thugs in my lab? I knew I should have hung onto that van until I had my stuff. Never should have let Joe talk me into trusting Luther to do the right thing."

After the hurricane, Myles had returned with Kendell and the band in Minerva's VW, which left Charlie, Joe, Delphine, and the professor to make their way back to New Orleans in the van stolen from Luther's operation.

"He was just trying to get the police off our backs," Myles said. "Had they decided we'd taken the van as a result of the post-hurricane confusion, we'd still be sitting in jail— all of us."

"Yeah, yeah. You don't have to remind me about the past. What really bugs me is Luther keeps hounding me to come to work for him. He got one look at my equipment, didn't have the foggiest idea of how it works, and convinced himself I would make the perfect addition to his operation. Like I'd ever be able to work in an office building."

"The abandoned World Trade Center is hardly an office building, but I get what you're saying. That's not why I'm here."

Professor Yates nodded like an academician considering a new theorem. "Where do I fit in?"

"Can you detect an object in another dimension? Specifically, we're still searching for Baron Samedi's cane, but if possible, it'd also be good to know that someone in this reality was keeping an eye on us. If Kendell carries the golden pick Papa Ghede gave her, could you track it?"

The professor turned to his gauges, paraphernalia, and metal boxes scattered around the room. Instead of offering the obvious excuse, he sighed. "Have her bring it by. I'll scan it. With any luck, I'll be able to build something from this ramshackle mess. At the very least, I should be able to tell if you're coming or going between dimensions."

Myles hated what he had to say next. "I'm going to leave you in charge. You'll be our main hope should things go wrong on the other side. Charlie's a good man—he's gotten me out of some tough scrapes—but he's not familiar with the dangers of our paranormal activities. Delphine is knowledgeable but useless in a fight. Plus, I still don't trust her. Joe Cazenave would have been my first choice, but I dare not approach him. Even if he weren't secretly trying to fix things from outside the department, he'd still need to maintain his cover. That, my friend, leaves you to watch our backs and rally the troops should things get hairy."

4

Colin sat on the wooden stairs of Scratch and Sniff, studying the rain. His observation started off with the drops not so much falling as looking as if they'd been fired out of a shotgun. Each drop exploded on impact with the ground. There wasn't a lot of water, but it fell with ferocity.

Three minutes and twenty seconds in—even though the minute and hour hands remained firmly at 6:52, he could still count how many times the second hand spun around the dial—a light breeze moved the walls of rain like air blowing a sheet dry on a clothesline. The wind blew some of the anger out of the storm. Colin beat the iron bar he'd used to break into the perfumery on the concrete curb to mark the change. The casual observer might hope the storm was finally moving off.

Of course, such a person, were there one, would be completely mistaken. After eleven minutes and forty-two seconds, the drops transformed from small vicious stinging pellets to large bomb-like balls that soaked everything they touched, like water balloons tossed from a window ten stories up.

He'd have happily spent the entire day in his study, but at twenty-seven minutes and fifty-four seconds, the cycle repeated. Even the storm was monotonous.

Staring at his watch wasn't his only means of telling how much time had passed. He rubbed his hand over his three-week-old beard. His cuts had healed, but his broken bones still ached. He found the physical improvement depressing. If he could heal, he could be hurt. And that meant he was probably not immortal. It was the one godlike power he had clung to.

He took a last look at his pocket watch before stashing it in his shirt. It was still 6:52 p.m. on Friday, July 18. He felt like a member of a theater audience when the movie reel was stuck on one frame. He'd stopped hoping someone would kick the projector. The witch's reality wasn't perfect, and that gave him an advantage, even if his body's functions deprived him of his divinity.

His analysis of time had revealed him to be in a dreamlike state. He couldn't sleep and never grew hungrier, but his wounds had healed, his broken bones were slowly mending, and of course, there was his beard. As for his environment, though the sky never changed from a constant dark gray and the rain only went through its twenty-eight-minute cycle, the vines that grew up the side of Delphine's shack showed progress in their attempts at covering the weathered wood. The elements might be stuck in a loop, but plants and animals lived by their own rules.

"What other truths do I know?"

Breaking into Delphine's shop confirmed that places he was connected to were more than just movie-set facades, but the bank office was still closed off to him. "What other buildings would be open to me?"

The Laurette mansion was a decent walk, especially in the frustratingly redundant storm, but he had little else to do. The walk from the swamp where the hurricane had left him had been much longer. As for being soaked and not having a functioning shower to help him clean up, it was only slightly more miserable than being dry.

He got up and turned toward the shop, searching for some shred of hope that he might have missed. Every one of her books might as well have been written in a foreign language—and many were. The curio cabinets and wall displays filled with voodoo relics weren't of much more use. In a fit of frustration, he'd considered smashing one or two, but releasing demons in hell seemed like a risky proposition.

"Okay, voodoo bitch, I'll be back when I know more."

As he stood, a rat scampered along the side of the porch. "Run on home, and tell your mistress where I am."

He stared after the retreating tail long after it had disappeared under the raised building. If people had occupied his hell, his first instinct would be to bend them to his desires. For the first time since entering this dimension, he kept his thoughts to himself. *Animals can be trained even easier than humans.*

At least without any people to bug him, he could hobble along under the balconies of the Quarter unimpeded and relatively dry. Once he passed the freeway overpass that divided the Warehouse District from the Lower Garden District, however, he was left at the mercy of the unrelenting rain. With every step, he wished the old swamp witch would change the weather channel. Even sweltering humidity would make a welcome change. Anything but the drudgery of dragging his body through the water that covered the streets and hid the unsuspecting potholes.

His expensive custom-made suit hung off his body like soaked dishrags that were beyond the rescue of a washing machine. He considered abandoning the societal demand for modesty. Who was there to care? But lurking somewhere in the shadows was Baron Samedi. Colin wouldn't give the voodoo loa the satisfaction of seeing him reduced to being hell's wild man. Even if the long coat were nothing more than shreds of silk lining, he'd meet his adversary as an equal.

The whereabouts of the witch was still a mystery. "With any luck, you're as bored as I am. You probably put this reality on repeat and walked away. Dumbest thing ever. You're like an old movie villain who doesn't stick around to see the hero's demise. That's your mistake, you know, because I'm going to figure a way out of here. If you never change anything about this reality, I will discover the weakness. If there isn't one, I'll find a spot and work on it until it comes free, just like this iron bar."

～

COLIN STOOD on the sidewalk and tried blinking the rain out of his eyes. Clearly, they weren't working properly. "It's too soon for me to have lost my mind." Making the statement didn't have any effect on the lights that shone from every window of the magnificent mansion.

"I'm going to have to give that construction foreman a raise. Not only did he get this job done in record time, but he must have also had the foresight to include a whole-house generator. You're losing, swamp witch. Do you hear me?"

In spite of the pain in his leg and side, he bounded up the varnished wood stairs to the covered porch that wrapped around the front of the building. The house he remembered from when he was a little boy had never looked this good. He doubted it had been this magnificent even when Baron Malveaux's son had completed it more than a hundred years earlier.

"I told you I'd possess your crowning achievement. Little punk, thinking you can deny me my family."

Continuing the condemnation, however, would only distract him from the lavish home he owned, even if it was in hell. He turned the gold-plated knob and shoved on the perfectly restored door with its cut-glass window.

The door remained shut.

"What the hell. This is *my* house."

The beveled glass distorted his view of the lavish interior, but someone was moving inside.

"Hey, you in there. Open the door." He pounded on the solid mahogany frame.

The door opened to reveal a beautiful woman in her

thirties. Her look of welcome quickly turned to the hard-eyed squint of someone greeting a door-to-door salesman. "I've been expecting you. We can talk in the foyer."

He wanted to push her aside and take possession of his mansion. However, she was the first person he'd seen in weeks, and his need for companionship outweighed his irritation at finding a squatter, no matter how upscale, in one of his buildings. "This is my house. Who are you?"

She motioned him toward an antique settee with a needlepoint cushion. As an accent, it wasn't bad. As a chair, it was barely functional. She stared at his eyes. "Who do you think I am?"

The azure blue of her eyes reminded him of the waters off the Virgin Islands.

"I'd have to guess you're some version of the old swamp witch. I see you've given yourself sight in this hell of mine."

"You're partially right. I'm acting as the interface between you and what the witch has created, but look again."

A stirring in his chest accompanied the softer lines around her eyes. He'd seen the unique color of azure before, and not as Lincoln Laroque. "That's not possible."

"I'm pleased you remember. With that jigsaw-puzzle soul of yours, I wasn't sure what you might retain."

Without meaning to, he was shaking his head. "No. That can't be. It's not possible." Her thin porcelain fingers reminded him of a doll he'd once purchased for her. "You're dead." The words came out as barely a whisper. "I spent a hundred and fifty years in Guinee searching for you."

"And what would you have done had you found me?

Kept me prisoner like those poor women you raped and forced to bear your children?"

He'd never felt judged before. Others had tried, but for him to accept their assessment, he would have had to care. "They were my companions."

"They were slaves, and you know it."

He reached over to touch her hand, but she snatched it away.

"I never meant to hurt you. I would have done anything to protect you."

"And yet you didn't. You'd been warned, but you didn't care."

"Serephine…" He hadn't used the name of his daughter since her death from the cursed pipe tool.

"You think I didn't know what you were up to? I wasn't even ten years old, but I knew. I loved you with all my heart before I found out. Once I did learn of how you'd treated those women in life, I wondered how it was even possible for you to love me."

"You and your brother—"

"Don't you even mention Antoine," she exclaimed with a ferocity that made him sit up straight. "He was the only one who cared about me. He built this mansion in my honor. Why else do you think I'm here?"

The stirring in his chest ignited a bonfire in his heart. His hope—which was not an emotion he accepted—was that she would keep him company in this hell. Even having her hate him was better than isolation. "You're here so I can apologize."

Her laugh still held vestiges of the child whose joy could

brighten even his worst day. But from the grown woman, the sarcastic tone cut him like a knife smoothly slicing into his heart. "I don't care about your guilt. You really have no clue, do you? I died as a child and made my way to the *deep waters* that are the home of humanity's shared soul."

The combatant who never left a boardroom in defeat began making his argument. "Reincarnation is not possible. I know. I've studied the subject. Once a person moves on to the *deep waters*, their soul is poured into the ocean to join everyone else's. You can't dip the same cup of water out of the ocean twice."

"You've studied your voodoo very well. But this realm isn't built on voodoo."

He shook his head. "Voodoo or Wicca, what's the difference? What a person believes doesn't matter. Reality is reality, no matter what we think."

"What we *believe* is all that matters. We make our own reality. You of all people should know that. You were the one who taught me that lesson. Or have you forgotten?"

Forcing him to relive the times he sat on the tapestry rug with his young daughter only increased his pain. "I was trying to give you my wisdom when I should have been learning yours."

"You still don't get it. Even after a century of watching the dead pass through your gate. Amazing."

He'd found the whining of the recently dead boring. They all complained about the same asinine thing: *If I only had more time.* "A person either uses the time they're given, or they don't. We're not immortal."

"And your answer was to ignore the only thing in life

that matters. *Love.* You didn't need to listen to me as a child —you needed to play with me. You needed to let me see who you were, not the hateful being you hid behind." She sighed in a way that let him know their time was nearly over. "But I guess that hidden person doesn't exist any longer. You became the mask you wore for the world."

He still had so many questions. "Why *are* you here?"

She looked around the elegantly appointed entry. "My life and this house are in another dimension—one not of your hell or the life you remember. In my world, my father loved me and did good things for the city of New Orleans. I grew up confident in myself and my sexuality, married a man who respects women, and had children. That's my reality. This hell is a space between dimensions. It's like a school hallway with doors that lead into classrooms." She pointed at the twelve-foot-high, intricately carved pocket doors to the living room. "When I return to my family, all this will go back to being the hallway. Do you understand now?"

He didn't want her to go. The idea that the beautiful mansion, and the woman who inhabited it, could vanish like turning off a light sent a panic into his heart. "You're the doorway. You guard the gate to the living the way I used to guard the seventh gate of Guinee."

She stood and offered him her hand. "You should go now. I have dinner to prepare and a family that needs me."

He longed to hug her, but he didn't know how. Instead he lifted her delicate hand to his lips and kissed it softly as a tear fell onto her perfect skin. "Will I see you again?"

"Only when you learn something meaningful."

He couldn't face seeing her leave. *Better to be the one walking out.* As he left the mansion, he noticed the rain had stopped. The clouds still covered the sky, but the blackness of night had replaced the gray late afternoon. The moon provided light and a sense of hope. He checked his pocket watch. It read 8:37. He stared at it for three cycles of the second hand, hoping the minute hand would continue to move. It didn't.

5

*M*yles did his best to understand what Professor Yates was doing to the old engine in the VW. Nothing made sense. The motor wasn't even where it should be in a normal car. Plus, it looked much too small to move the bus. With all the paraphernalia the quack inventor had jerry-rigged around the engine bay, the compartment looked uncomfortably like the old man's lab. "And this is going to make the bus go faster?"

"You don't need to understand it. I just want you to remember where everything goes in case one of the connections falls off in the transfer from this reality to the next."

Myles feared there wouldn't be a demonic mechanic on the other side, though he wasn't really sure a living grease monkey would have much more luck with the air-cooled engine. He looked up at Kendell, hoping she was having better luck with Delphine. The way his girlfriend kept tapping her notebook with her pen, between writing things down, left him to believe they might be looking at a one-way trip to hell.

She returned his worried look. "I guess we'd better find that cane."

"You know your way around a spell, and I've got at least one loa friend where we're headed. We'll get by."

Minerva had her head poking up out of the sunroof of the bus as the other band members handed up their instruments. "Don't worry about my old girl. She's yet to strand me anywhere. There have been some roadside repairs, but we have an understanding. Of course, if anyone had an HAA card, that'd be cool."

"What?" Kendell had her waiting-for-the-punch-line look.

"Hell Automobile Association."

Lynn struggled to get her keyboard up the side of the van. "Yeah, or the number of Demonic Towing Company."

"We'll drive you from hell," Scraper added.

Myles wasn't sure the occasion called for levity, but it beat focusing on the task at hand. As everyone else found their seats, he waited, hoping it was just his imagination that the narrow tires looked to be bulging. He handed Cheesecake to Kendell in the back seat before squeezing through the sliding door to join them.

The professor explained his modification to Minerva, who was sitting behind the wheel. "Just lay into the accelerator. I've changed out the oil to handle higher RPMs and given the gas a bit of an octane boost. She might balk a bit after shifting."

Delphine added, "For the spell to work, you'll need to get fully up to speed then shift into fifth gear."

Minerva didn't look impressed by the work others had done to her pride and joy. "There is no fifth gear."

"With the silver skull, there is. Just get it moving and shift, trusting it's there."

"So long as you don't tell me to get her up to eighty-eight miles per hour. This is a Volkswagen, not a DeLorean. The engine isn't the only limiting factor. For aerodynamic reasons, these old buses were never turned into hotrods."

Delphine didn't seem concerned, but then, it wasn't her butt sitting on top of the little engine that could. "Take the Crescent City Connection across the river. I've put a traffic jam spell on the freeway, so you'll have the straight stretch of road to yourself. With Professor Yates's modifications, you should be able to make the climb with little trouble. Once you get to the top, put it in fifth and give it all you've got. Downhill with the wind behind you should be enough to blast you to the other side."

Professor Yates patted the side of the van. "We'll be keeping an eye on you from this side."

"Like that's going to do any good." Myles grumbled so low he hoped even Kendell hadn't heard him.

The way Professor Yates and Delphine backed away from the bus before Minerva started the engine didn't inspire confidence. The little four-cylinder engine sputtered as though it had been given prune juice after a lifetime of drinking wine.

"Come on, girl. I know you've got it in you." Minerva

caressed the steering wheel before giving it another shot of battery life.

A loud explosion emanated from the tailpipe, followed by a rattling behind the bench seat Myles shared with Kendell, Sanguine, and Cheesecake.

Minerva pumped the gas. The hyped-up engine rocked the bus to the side as it experienced far more power than it had been designed to handle.

Cheesecake snuggled tightly to the laps of Kendell and Myles.

"One way or another, we're leaving this plane of existence." Myles's lame joke managed to get a smattering of nervous laughs from the women.

"What do you say we give first gear a try?" Minerva let out the clutch.

The rattling of water bottles and other garbage left under the bench seats announced the bus was in gear. As if getting ready for a Disney ride, Myles hoped everyone's arms were inside the vehicle.

The bus struggled through the city streets. With every stoplight, the people in the van held their breath. Minerva couldn't find the sweet spot between the clutch and accelerator. Each start was like being launched out of cannon—a quick start followed by an unnerving hesitation when Myles wasn't sure if the bus would make it to the next gear.

He breathed a little easier as the overloaded VW flew up the on-ramp. With no other cars around, Minerva gave the old vehicle all the gas it could take. From the smell in the back of the bus, Myles suspected flames were shooting out of the tailpipes.

Like a sports car that was finally being driven at its proper speed, the old bus ran through the gears at high RPMs. The small engine still had the putter of the old VW, but at the much higher RPMs, it sounded as if it was on steroids.

Kendell held Cheesecake tightly in her lap. "If this is going slow, I'm worried about what happens when we crest the bridge. I feel like I'm on a rollercoaster and kind of want to get off before I go over the edge. Maybe this wasn't such a good idea."

"I don't recall anyone thinking this was a *good* idea." Myles kept his arm around her as the asphalt road in the windshield disappeared.

"Here goes nothing." Minerva threw the bus into the mystical fifth gear.

Even Scraper, in the passenger seat, was screaming as the bus doubled its speed on the downhill run toward the Westbank.

In the blink of an eye, the bright summer day turned to night. Water covered the roadway, and the bus was skidding wildly out of control.

"Hit the brakes!" Scraper yelled as she grasped the handle on the dash.

"Can't. I'll lose all traction. I've got this."

Myles admired Minerva's confidence. Were he driving, he was pretty sure they'd be headed over the side of the bridge. As the roadway leveled out, she took the first exit and let the incline of the overpass slow the bus's momentum.

"Piece of cake."

Cheesecake growled at Minerva, but Myles wasn't sure if it was due to the reference or her driving.

In the past, Myles's mental journeys to the afterlife had the advantage of instantaneous travel. Getting around in an unknown realm had never been an issue.

The bus rolled to a stop at the end of the off-ramp. "Okay, navigators, where to?"

"Make a left," Kendell said. "Head out toward the river. I'm not ready to face Colin the Devil just yet. We need to get our bearings."

The nicely paved roadway that cut through the parklike setting wasn't what Myles had expected. "I've only come over here by ferry, but I thought there were a lot more houses over here."

Looking at Sanguine, Myles thought, *She's fidgeting in her seat like a girl who's about to visit her grandparents*. He realized the comparison wasn't that far off. "What you see while we're here isn't completely based on the reality we know. My grandmother created this realm to conform to the inhabitants."

Kendell petted Cheesecake's head. The act helped both of them remain calm. "I don't understand. What inhabitants?"

Sanguine turned away from the window. "The curse is the foundation for this reality. There are now two people in this world who are connected to the environment—you and Colin Malveaux. He's the fulfillment of the curse's objective, so this place is meant to teach him a lesson. You, however, are the ultimate beneficiary—the inheritor, as Marie Laveau put it. Imagine what would have happened if there'd been no need for the curse."

Kendell leaned back on the bench seat and stared out the window. "For Louis Broussard not to have commissioned the curse, he would have needed to be able to pay back Baron Malveaux and the bank. So his invention for draining the swamp worked?"

Sanguine closed her eyes as if slipping into a trance. "As the new swamp witch, I can call up any version of the past. His creation didn't help his agricultural experiment. This land, though productive, never made him much money. However, the ability to remove large volumes of water efficiently became the foundation for the city's flood control. Many hurricanes that in our reality flooded the city were quickly drained thanks to Louis Broussard." She opened her eyes. "It's kind of like being a tour guide. Each time we experience a change in reality, I'll be able to digest the CliffsNotes on what happened."

"Cool," Kendell said. "So this area would be the home to his descendants in this reality. And presumably, they'd be well off, thanks to what he did for the city. So far, hell doesn't sound so bad from my perspective."

"It's not your hell—just an alternate reality. You'll want to be very clear on that point. If you focus on something here, even if it's something you want to avoid, it will become your reality. My grandmother used to say, 'Where you look is where you go.' She meant if you fixate on something, you end up making it happen."

Myles understood the concept. "Right. So no imagining burning sulfur pits, only sunshine and puppies."

"Simplistic, but not wrong. It's not just about the surroundings, though. There are countless alternate realities. Each is completely true to the people who inhabit it. So the people you meet over here aren't illusions. They're very real. As with the curse itself, Kendell is a doorway between dimensions."

"So we'll see a completely different New Orleans?" Kendell asked.

"Not quite. We haven't jumped into that new dimension. We're only standing at the doorway. It'll take someone from the other side who's equally open to the mystical for you to establish the link."

Minerva swung the bus off the main road onto an avenue shaded on both sides by oak trees. "I saw a house down here with its lights on. Seemed like a good place to start our investigation."

Despite its long driveway, the plantation house wasn't particularly grand or imposing. The single-story home with the wraparound porch looked well maintained, modest, and inviting.

"Who do you think lives here?" Myles asked.

As the bus rolled to a stop, Kendell was struggling out of her seat before Lynn had the sliding door open. "I could hazard a guess."

It took Myles a moment to realize the woman running down the porch was the same Mary who, in their reality, was the matriarch of the homeless community who lived on the batture. This version of the woman was thinner, wore a flowing dress instead of the tattered housecoat he remembered, and was clearly a woman of means. She embraced Kendell as she got out of the van. "I've been expecting you."

"But how?" Kendell asked.

"My silly angel, don't you remember Whit telling you I was a *seer*?"

Though the ride had only been from one side of the river to the other, Myles felt as if he'd been crammed in the bus for days. He stretched out his back as he looked around the riverfront plantation. "Even with Sanguine's explanation, I'm still not clear on how you know us without Kendell knowing anything about your life."

"A person can only face one direction," Mary explained. "I'm standing here, in this in-between reality, focusing on where you've come from. To do that, I have to suspend my connection to my reality."

Kendell continued to hold Mary tight. "It doesn't matter. I'm just so happy to know there's a reality out there where you're the inheritor of this land."

Mary looked over the group. "Bring your things. There are plenty of bedrooms. So long as I'm in this space, you'll all be welcome. I'll stay as long as you need me."

Sanguine stopped in front of the woman. "Do you know why we're here?"

"I know enough. Get some rest. We'll talk in the morning."

∼

MARY KEPT her arm tightly around Kendell's waist as they walked along the batture. Across the river, the remains of Hurricane Agnes continued to threaten the Quarter and would for the foreseeable future. But on the Westbank, it was a calm, sunny day as if it were in the eye of the storm.

Kendell needed answers but wasn't sure Mary would be able to provide anything other than a place of peace. "As a seer, what can you tell me about this reality?"

The woman who felt more like a mother to Kendell than her own mom looked out at the river. "It's not stable, but I'm not sure it was meant to be. I'm only an observer here. You, however, are actually present in this strange place. That gives you power to change things." She looked back at Kendell. "I suppose that's not very helpful. In my world, there are so many people that what we know of as reality is pretty consistent. The more people, the less deviation. Though your friends are with you, they don't have the power to change things like you do."

"And Colin Malveaux has that same power?"

"I don't know. Time doesn't make much sense here, and that confuses what I see." She pointed across the river. "You see how it's still dark and gloomy over there, like nothing has changed since last night? While you've been here, we've gone from night into day. If Colin has power over his environment, I don't think he's discovered it yet."

Cheesecake ran through the tall grass like a dog half her age. It warmed Kendell's heart to see the old girl having so much fun.

That feeling flipped to terror when Cheesecake came to an abrupt halt ten feet in front of her. The dog lifted her droopy ears as high as she could, a clear sign she'd heard something that put her on edge.

"What is it, girl?" After Cheesecake's abduction, Kendell swore to never again take any of the dog's reactions for granted.

The pup tore across the field with a growl that made Kendell break into a run without thinking. Ahead, a dense thicket of vines and reeds bordered the river. Certain there was either a gator or some other terror from the Mississippi lurking along the shore, Kendell screamed for her dog to stop, but Cheesecake wasn't listening. She dove paws first into the vegetation.

Between the fear and exertion, Kendell's heart felt ready to explode. She could hear Cheesecake growling in the reeds, but other than the bushes shaking, she couldn't identify the threat.

Before Kendell reached the water's edge, Cheesecake emerged from the brush and trotted up to her, looking far too pleased with herself.

"What the hell was that about? You nearly gave me a heart attack."

Cheesecake sat at attention in front of her and let out a solitary *arf*.

The bushes behind the dog began to shake. Kendell braced herself for some demonic creature from hell to emerge.

Instead of the dreaded fear-inducing demon, a brown-and-white puppy ran out from the reeds, giving her little legs all she had to pounce up to Cheesecake. The ball of fur landed on her belly at the bigger dog's side.

"Oh my god. That is the cutest dog ever."

But Cheesecake didn't give Kendell long to admire the little girl. She let out two very distinct *arf*s.

A brindle pup with curly hair ran out of the plants so fast she lost her footing and did a tail-over-head somersault. She stood back up and shook the blades of grass out of her face. It took the dog a moment to figure out where she was headed. Again, she ran much too fast and ended up plowing headfirst into Cheesecake's tail. The old girl turned her head to the pup, grabbed her by the mane, and positioned her on the side opposite her sister.

Without waiting for Kendell's response, Cheesecake let out three *arf*s. Kendell once again thought her heart was about to explode, but this time it was out of happiness instead of fear.

Nothing happened in the weeds. Cheesecake remained facing Kendell but gave a solid growl before repeating her three *arf*s.

There was still no response from the plants.

Cheesecake stood up, faced the brush, and gave her fiercest growl, normally reserved for when Kendell had failed to provide dinner on time.

Finally, the weeds parted and a black-and-tan pup ran out onto the grassy field. He got halfway before stopping and shaking the river water and mud from his coat. As he stood at attention, Kendell could see that the tan coloring was actually just dirt.

Cheesecake resumed her seat between the cute little balls of fluff. The canine newcomer behind her looked crestfallen. Kendell wanted so badly to rush over and pick him up, but she had to trust that her dog was the one in charge. The little guy let out a pathetic whimper and ran full speed until he was at the front of the pack. Then he sat down between Cheesecake's front paws.

Kendell turned to Mary. "How in the world is this even possible? Clearly, they're her puppies, but I do know a thing or two about how animals get pregnant and have offspring. Does she have puppies in your reality?"

Mary looked as enamored with the little dogs as Kendell was. "I've never seen any of these dogs in my life."

Having introduced her brood, Cheesecake got up and started running across the field but with her head turned back so she could watch her puppies chasing after her. Kendell had never seen her dog so happy. Unable to keep up, the little mites chased after their mother, yipping and howling. Having teased them sufficiently, Cheesecake doubled back and rolled onto her back. The hellions jumped, ran, and nipped at their mother while she wriggled around in the grass.

"I don't get it. How can she have puppies?"

Mary wrapped her arm around Kendell. "It's what I was trying to explain. Every animal develops its own reality. With so many people around us, we have to fit our sense of identity into the bigger picture like pieces of a puzzle. And as humans, we're bound to logical thinking. Cheesecake isn't tied to our strict rules of existence. In this reality, there aren't any other dogs, so she gets to choose to be whoever she wants. Clearly, she wanted to be a mom."

~

MYLES WATCHED the women sitting in a circle on the antique braided rug, playing with the puppies. Kendell looked up at him. "We need to name them. Don't you think? Or do you worry I'll get too attached to them if they have names?"

He knew it might not be all that manly, but he couldn't resist the puppy cuteness. "Like you're not already attached to them? I don't see any harm in giving them names. It's not like we can *arf* for them like their mama."

She wasted no time in snatching up the brindle little girl. "This one's Muffin Top. I always liked those pumpkin-spice muffins we serve at the coffeehouse, so she her nickname can be Pumpkin. What do you think?"

For the briefest moment, Myles thought she was talking to him, but from the way she held the little dog up for Cheesecake's inspection, she was clearly seeking the mom's approval. Cheesecake gave kisses to both the puppy and Kendell.

"Good. I thought you'd approve." She picked up the brown-and-white girl. "And I thought Cupcake for this one. She has your markings, but instead of black, hers are brown. So I thought Cake would be a good way to honor that connection. I'll call her Cuppers when we're playing."

Again Cheesecake signaled that she liked the name by giving her traditional single bark then kissing both Kendell and Cupcake.

Myles felt a bond with the little dude. The boy pup was outnumbered by the females. Myles feared the women would give him some cutesy name like Beignet. "I like Doughnut Hole for that little guy."

61

Both Cheesecake and Kendell looked at him as though he'd lost his mind.

"Why are you being an ass?" Kendell said.

He seldom understood what Kendell would find irritating, but apparently, he had a remarkable ability to hit on it without trying. "What's wrong with doughnut holes? They're small and cute and kind of squishy."

"Do not squeeze that dog."

Her anger made him laugh. "Like I would ever hurt him. What do you think, Cheesecake?"

The old girl stared up at Kendell with a look of aggravation. The small black puppy, however, pranced between the women and started licking Myles's hand with such ferocity that neither Kendell nor Cheesecake could object to the name.

"So what are you going to call him when you're playing? Please don't say something stupid like Dough Hole, or I swear I'll make you change the name."

He held the dog up to look it in the face. "Nope. He's Hell Hole. At least when he's bad. We'll work on something else for you to call him. What do you say, boy?"

The squirmy dude kissed Myles's nose.

Polly snuggled Muffin Top to her face. "She feels so real. But if she's not part of our reality, and not part of Mary's, what happens when we leave?"

It wasn't a question Myles had wanted to ask. Kendell looked at Sanguine. "Please tell me they don't just poof into thin air."

Sanguine shook her head. "This place may be between dimensions, but it's still very real. No matter how these little ones came into existence, they are very much a part of this place. The real question is, what are you going to do with them?"

Mary sat in the antique rocking chair. "I can take them with me. The door to my reality will change them slightly. I'm not sure how. Being hounds from hell, they might manifest as actual hound dogs or big water dogs. You can rest assured they'll be well loved."

From the way Kendell pulled the little pups to her, Myles could tell she wouldn't turn them loose voluntarily. She was almost as possessive of the little creatures as Cheesecake was. "We'll cross that dimensional bridge when we get to it. There's still a loa of the dead to rescue, a magical cane to find, and a devil to contain."

6

$\mathcal{K}$endell snuggled against Myles on the porch swing. "Have you had any thoughts on where to find Baron Samedi?" She loved the way the little pups lay at her feet next to Cheesecake.

"The most logical answer would be New Orleans Bank and Trust, where Baron Malveaux had his seventh gate to Guinee. The thing is, if Baron Samedi is trapped on this side, that door between realms might be stuck open. I keep thinking about something Mary said regarding the puppies. If beings cross from one reality into another, they may not be the same. Cheesecake has already proven she can appear as a she-wolf in other dimensions. If we're careless in how we approach Baron Samedi, we might inadvertently provide an access between the two worlds, thereby giving Colin a way to escape. Who knows what kind of a devil he'd be in Guinee."

She nodded against his chest. "Not to mention those dead souls trying to get through Guinee to the *deep waters*. Instead of finding peace, they could end up trapped in hell."

"All the more reason for Baron Samedi to be standing guard at the gate until it's sealed, but this hell isn't his realm. Papa Ghede said Colin could be learning to be a god in this custom-built reality. If he gets hold of the cane, Baron Samedi could be in real trouble."

Holding him close helped her face the dangers. "We could try to capture Colin, but he's had time to make this reality his home turf. We really don't know what we're up against."

"First, we need Samedi's help to combat Colin." Myles liked to list things, especially when they were at the beginning of a paranormal mission. "We're going to need to find that cane too. Then, according to Sanguine and Delphine, there's a gate from his hell to our reality. Even though we didn't go through an actual location to get here, we must have been allowed to pass by some guardian. We need to find out who's in charge. That access is the real problem. Once we have it secured, we need to make sure the loa escapes to Guinee and seals the gate shut so Colin can't follow. And finally, we'll need to get home ourselves without Colin following us."

She leaned down and petted Cheesecake's back. The dog looked up at her with a look of supreme contentment.

"That's a lot of running around while hoping Colin doesn't notice us. It's not like we're going to have Joe's paramilitary force watching our backs. We'll be on our own this time. And don't forget, I need to reinforce this existence. According to Delphine, Colin needs something to keep him occupied so he doesn't continue trying to bust down the walls of hell. I don't even know how to identify the problems over here. This is beginning to sound like a lost cause."

"Bullshit. Nothing's a lost cause unless we let it be one. I like the way Mary put it: where you look is where you go."

She disturbed Cheesecake and her sleeping pups when she got off the swing. Standing on the edge of the porch, she looked across the river. "Where do you think Colin is right now?"

"My guess would be his penthouse office. I see him as an evil despot in his tower, looking over his domain. Even if he thinks there's no one else in his reality, he'd want the highest perch possible to keep an eye out for intruders."

She nodded. "That's what I figure too. Running around in Minerva's bus is going to call attention to us being here, but I can't come up with a reasonable alternative."

"So we lose the advantage of a sneak attack, but we'll have mobility on our side. The best thing we can do is move fast."

Other than seeing the next move, she'd never been much good at figuring out a strategy. "We also outnumber him. How can we utilize that strength?"

"We need a plan."

"The first thing would be to talk to Baron Samedi," Kendell said, "but I don't imagine we'll be able to just stroll into the bank's main office."

"I suspect he's set up a barrier to prevent Colin from

doing just that. If we can get into the bank, I'd take it as a good sign. You and I can head over in the morning, or at least what we perceive as morning."

Cheesecake was never a fan of sitting by herself. She nudged the pups awake before joining Kendell on the stoop.

"That leaves Sanguine and the band to scout out the Quarter," Kendell said. "We need to know the lay of the land."

"No one would understand this hell better than Sanguine. She can coordinate the band's efforts."

Kendell sat down among the dogs. "Eventually we're going to have to confront Colin, and probably sooner rather than later. I'd assume he's still wearing the cursed items. Maybe I can figure out what he's up to."

Myles always gave her flack when she connected to Colin. "Are you sure that's such a good idea? Sanguine said if you relied too much on that connection, you might end up opening your soul to him. Trust me, that's not something you want to happen—especially here."

She couldn't face him when talking about putting herself at risk. His look of concern had a way of melting her resolve. "You're right, but we need to know our arsenal. Using my connection may be a last resort, but it's a strength we can't ignore."

"It's only a strength if you can mentally defeat him. I tried and failed."

"You were on your own. I should have been able to help, but I did the opposite." She held herself responsible for Myles's possession and would do so no matter what he said.

"This isn't the time for self-recrimination."

She turned from the puppies to him. "That's not what I'm saying. You can access my soul with your psychometric ability, and you've been able to bring Delphine and even Cheesecake along. Imagine the joint force of everyone here funneled through my being. Colin wouldn't stand a chance."

"It's the hidden dangers that worry me. We don't know what that would do to you."

He had a point. Hell probably wasn't the best place to further her voodoo skills. "So we have the advantage of numbers, but he has us when it comes to accessing this hell's paranormal characteristics."

"We have Sanguine. You're connected to Colin through the curse, but this reality is in her blood."

∾

THE BAND and Sanguine listened attentively to the plan for the day, but Kendell could tell from their body language that they weren't thrilled with once again be relegated to reconnaissance.

"And what if Colin steals my van and drives it back to the living?" Minerva asked.

Sanguine sighed and explained for the umpteenth time about her grandmother's creation. "It doesn't work that way. We got here because the silver skull was a part of Baron Samedi's cane. The skull and cane are like two magnets that snapped together and are now stuck in the same realm."

Polly looked pissed. "Wait. Are you saying this was a

one-way trip? Seems like someone could have mentioned that before we loaded into the bus."

"Would it have stopped you?" Kendell asked. "You seemed pretty insistent on coming with me. Don't worry. We all have people in life to welcome us back. All Sanguine meant was the bus isn't going to do Colin any good. He's got no one left in life, so he's got no bridge back to the living."

Sanguine had a habit of making people crazy first, then explaining later. "Even if he did, my grandmother set this place up as an isolation unit for his soul. He can't connect, so he can't escape. The other dimensions are closed to him. As you can see from this plantation, Kendell can cross into other dimensions. When the time comes, we'll get out of here."

Polly seemed to relax a bit from the explanation. "In that case, seeing as how we're the only people in this reality, maybe we could take the opportunity to set up our equipment in whatever passes for the Scratchy Dog. If we're going to be over there anyway, we might as well get a jam session in."

"We're trying to keep a low profile," Myles said.

Kendell knew eventually she'd need to pull out her inner voodoo priestess even if he disagreed. "It's not a bad idea, though. I need to find out what I can do over here. A little gig might prove instructive. We're not going to stay hidden for long."

Mary stood in the doorway of the comfortable plantation home. "I can't go with you. This property is the extent of my connection. I'll keep an eye on the dogs until you return. With Cheesecake here, Kendell will have her link to my reality."

Kendell knew Cheesecake didn't belong on the other side of the river. It was too dangerous. Plus, she had her puppies to look after. "It'll be okay, girl. I'll be back as soon as I can."

With everyone loaded up, Kendell looked longingly back at Mary, who stood on the porch with the dogs. Being a mother figure with a plantation to look after wasn't a life Kendell had wanted, but Mary had a way of making it look good. "Did you ever think about having children?"

She could feel Myles tense up next to her. "We just moved in together, and already you're talking about kids?"

"No, I didn't mean *I* wanted them. But I never imagined Cheesecake felt there was something missing in her life. Had I known, I would have found a way for her to have puppies."

He put his arm around her. "We find love in the strangest of places."

As the bus crept up onto the freeway, Minerva called out from the driver's seat. "I'm going to keep it to third gear. I don't want any unexpected other-dimensional off-ramps showing up. The most direct route to the club would be to pass by the convention center. It's only a couple of blocks from Colin's office, but it's not like there's a more surreptitious way into the Quarter."

"You can drop us off at Jackson Square," Myles said. "No need to drive around looking for trouble."

"Just think of me as your demonic Uber driver." Minerva

maneuvered the old bus through the still-flooded streets as if it were an amphibious military vehicle.

Myles jumped out first then helped Kendell out of the bus at the wrought-iron gates where horse-drawn carriages usually awaited passengers. "First impressions?"

The sense of calm she felt was almost eerie. "Have you ever been in a sensory-deprivation tank?"

"No."

Her skin tingled as if from static electricity. "Then my explanation might not make much sense, but I have the same feeling now."

"My senses are on full alert, so you're going to have to come up with a better explanation."

Kendell's feeling of aloneness grew as Minerva drove off. "Usually when I'm in the Quarter, there are so many people that I feel cocooned by their energy. I know that some find the crowds claustrophobic, but being surrounded by a happy population makes me feel like I'm in a warm blanket."

He nodded. "You're describing what I feel when I'm floating in the *deep waters*."

"Exactly. A deprivation tank is so quiet I feel like I'm filling the chamber with my very being. I fear this realm is trying to suck at my soul like a desert sucking up a glass of spilled water."

He pointed toward the far corner of the park. "Let's get to the bank. Once I'm inside a structure, maybe I'll get a better idea of what you're experiencing."

They dodged the largest puddles, but the walk still soaked Kendell's Keds and the cuffs of her jeans. "I'm glad you talked me into wearing pants, but you could have pushed harder on the rain boots."

"Complain to Sanguine. How was I to know we'd be stuck in the aftermath of hurricane Agnes?"

Though water flowed into the catch basins, the level in the street didn't seem to be going down. "At least the rain's stopped."

Myles held her hand as they climbed the rain-slick steps to the bank. He pushed open the ten-foot-tall doors. Dried footsteps on the Italian marble floor indicated they weren't the first to visit the institution. "One guess about who those belong to."

Kendell was relieved to see that the shoeprints went both directions. "Colin isn't stupid. I'd guess this was his first stop too."

"Let's hope Baron Samedi is relying on more than the flooded streets for his protection." He rubbed his hands along his bare arms.

"I know we got a little wet, but late July doesn't usually make you cold."

"I'm not cold. The mental isolation is exactly the same feeling I had while being possessed by Baron Malveaux."

She shivered at his explanation. "Completely cut off from all living souls."

"Not quite. This place is connected to Colin Malveaux. It's part of his reality and no one else's."

She remembered sneaking in with Delphine to offer the libation at the seventh gate prior to Myles's exorcism. "The office is on the third floor. It's hard to miss."

Intermixed with the dried-sole prints ascending the

stairs were slide marks indicating Colin had needed help. The corresponding descending marks of shoes and walking stick were much more distinct, as was the butt mark where he'd sat.

"Looks like he was in a hurry getting to the office but not as excited about leaving," Myles said.

As they walked down the empty third-floor corridor, all Kendell saw was a smooth plaster wall where the ornately carved door had been. "I don't understand. Where is it?"

"I think we just discovered why no one's seen Baron Samedi lately. So is he holding the gate shut, or is he trapped in there?"

She reached into her back pocket and pulled out the golden guitar pick. "Only one way to find out." She laid it on her open palm and faced the wall.

The pick flew out of her hand and embedded in the wall like an arrowhead penetrating an animal's hide, but instead of blood dripping from the resultant wound, the wall exploded like thin, tempered glass.

The door was exactly as she remembered it. "Should we knock?"

He stepped up to the carved mahogany frame and turned the knob, like a child trying to sneak into his father's office. "Either he's not here, or he's expecting us."

Baron Samedi sat behind the oversized desk, looking pale and emaciated—not a good look for a loa of the dead. "I'm glad it's you."

"What happened?" Myles asked.

The loa of the dead struggled to sit upright. "The old swamp witch's hurricane didn't work on me the way it did on Colin Malveaux. I'm spirit, not flesh. As she was Wiccan, her energy separated me from my voodoo realm, but this seventh gate exists across all dimensions. Think of it as a foreign embassy. Each religion that Papa Ghede spun off maintains diplomatic ties to the other. Unfortunately, because of how that old witch set up Colin's jail cell, I got stuck in this room. Guinee relies on connections to people and the *deep waters*. This office is like a freshwater pond on an island in a lake cut off from the ocean, and I'm a saltwater fish. Understand?"

"All too well," Myles said. "How do we get you back to where you belong?"

"Finding my cane would be a good start."

Kendell had been certain Baron Samedi had it with him. "I don't understand. If Colin doesn't have it—which seems unlikely since he would have had a lot more sway in this reality if he did—and it's not among the living, where is it?"

"As my staff is from Guinee, it probably suffered the same fate as I did. But it's not here at the seventh gate."

Myles began pacing the room. "This isn't the only gate to Guinee, though. If all seven are connected like embassies, it might have ended up in one of the other cemeteries."

"We need to find it. The girls can spread out and start searching the cemeteries." The cane being loose somewhere Colin could get to it had been one of Kendell's worst fears.

Myles was still pacing in front of the desk. "All that activity might only alert Colin to the fact that it's not in this room. If Baron Samedi was called here to the bank, the cane might have also found its way to where it was most connected."

Kendell loved following his line of reasoning. "Of course, Marie Laveau's tomb. It's the first gate."

Baron Samedi put his long bony fingers together. "Because its essence is trapped here, it may not have substance. In order for us to use it, you'll need to make it real for you. I hope you made a thorough study of Marie's journal. And you're going to need that silver skull."

7

*C*olin stalked his desk like a CEO planning a hostile takeover. Finally, he picked up the radius bone that was still attached to the skeletal fingers grasping the cane and shook it. "Let go of my walking stick, you fucking devil voodoo bitch!"

Early in his captivity, he'd hallucinated quite a lot. He couldn't be sure, but he thought he saw the middle-finger bones extend out from the cane then wrap back around the stick.

"Maybe it's better that you hang onto it. Swamp witch only knows what would happen if you let go. I certainly can't grab it. It'd probably just fall straight through the building's floors to another form of hell."

He tossed the bones holding the hologram-like cane back on his desk. "At least those pesky kids won't get their hands on it."

The dull glow around the buildings on the far side of the

Quarter indicated the location of the hellish VW with the band of women. He longed to confront them, but he feared relinquishing the upper hand. This was his realm. His only real competition, Baron Samedi, was isolated in his office fortress. The swamp witch, like most deities, didn't deign to make herself known.

That only left Serephine in the old mansion. For weeks, he'd made the pilgrimage from the Central Business District to the Garden District on the off chance that she might see him again. Each time, the mansion looked like a corpse with the flesh falling from its bones. Great gaping holes in the siding revealed the studs without the internal walls. In places, he could see straight through the structure to the vine-covered backyard.

The place depressed him, but not because of the forever-arrested state of disrepair. A reality existed in which his daughter was busy living her life, and he had no part in it except as a memory she kept hidden away like some ex-lover's pain-filled letters.

"Fuck her. If I'm the devil here, I might as well embrace the role. Those kids were fools to stumble into my domain. They will pay the price." He turned back to the bones on his desk. "You hear me, voodoo queen? You may have your precious magic wand, but you can't protect the insects that fly into my web."

All of his bravado, however, didn't change the fact this was no longer only his realm. Finding the cane had been simple enough. After all, Marie Laveau had been a longtime resource for keeping Archibald Malveaux's adversaries in check, so when she originally approached him with the idea of stealing the cane from Baron Samedi, he'd listened. As the most powerful banker in the city, and the primary patron for New Orleans's first Mardi Gras parade, he'd been one of the few to ride on the grand marshal's float. What no one knew was that Baron Samedi was also on that float. Snatching the cane had taken little more skill than that of a common pickpocket.

But Marie hadn't meant for him to keep the magical cane. Foolishly, she thought she was using him. Figuring out that the stick had run home to Mama, he'd chosen her tomb as one of the first places he'd vandalized.

But seeing the vintage VW driving down Convention Center Drive—now, that had come as a surprise. Time hadn't meant a damn thing, but with someone else in his realm, it would be a race to see who could control the cane first. Possessing it gave him the clear advantage, but he'd made no progress since getting it and the bones back to his office.

"I suppose it's back to your great-granddaughter's shop and all your mysterious books."

Waiting would only give those damn kids a chance to catch up. Having the advantage only worked if he kept one step ahead and didn't use it as an excuse to sit back and coast.

~

"Looks like we're too late." Kendell pulled a couple more bricks from the bashed-in front of the aboveground crypt.

Myles peered around her into the deathly darkness. "I

think she put up a fight. Look at the top of the casket. Looks like something tried to bust out. There's wood splinters all over the place."

Kendell had never been afraid of dead things, and her time studying voodoo only heightened her understanding that the wall between the living and the dead wasn't as solid as many suspected. She lifted the lid in the house of the dead. "She's missing an arm bone at the elbow. The way the rest of the bones project toward the lid of the coffin makes me think she was reaching for something. I'd have to believe that would be the cane."

"Even in death, she's got a hankering for it. I'll be glad to see it returned to Guinee, where it belongs."

Kendell knew enough of the story to believe Marie Laveau wouldn't have wanted the inheritor of Baron Malveaux's soul to once again possess her voodoo prize. "I doubt it would do her any good now. My guess is she put some spell on her crypt to somehow snatch the cane if possible."

"Since the only person in this reality is Colin Malveaux, we don't need three guesses to figure out who has it. But this hell still seems the way Sanguine described it, so though he might have it, he must not know how to use it."

Kendell felt the stirrings of hope. "Baron Samedi said we'd need to make it part of our reality. What if the reason she's missing an arm is because he can't handle it? He'd need to find answers, but he wouldn't know we have the curse diary regarding the cane. The last time he would have seen the book would be in Delphine's lap as she read the passage about removing the silver skull while Sanguine and I performed our magic. She didn't give me the journal until after he left to chase Sanguine."

Myles leaned against the tomb. "So our next stop is Scratch and Sniff?"

Kendell thought they might finally be one step ahead of their adversary. "He'll assume we'll be searching for the same answers. If he pursues us, we might be able to set a trap. At the very least, we could find something voodooish to use against him."

As they walked the handful of blocks from the cemetery to the shop, she tried to imagine what Colin might have done with his time in hell. Certainly a trip to Scratch and Sniff would have been high on the list of places he'd go for answers, but she wondered if he could even enter the building. Between it being Delphine's shop and filled with Marie's work, there had to be some powerful voodoo protection spells to ward off any intruder. However, this wasn't the voodoo realm. Had Kendell been in his position, she'd have carefully boxed up all of the writings and transported them to her lair for intense study, but Colin didn't strike her as the book-nerd type. Assuming he was able to get past the front door, his irritation at not being able to decode the writings would have set off a fit of rage. The journals were hard enough for her to figure out under the guidance of Delphine.

Myles pointed at the hole in Scratch and Sniff's front door where the doorknob had been. "Looks like we're not the first ones to come here for answers. You'd better let me go in to check things out."

Though she firmly believed in female equality, she didn't

see the harm in a little male chivalry from time to time. "Just be careful."

He stood still for a moment. "What would that look like —being careful, I mean? We're in hell, and I'm about to walk into a voodoo shop that the devil probably frequented."

"Don't be an ass, or I'll go first."

He gave her a kiss on the cheek. "For luck."

MYLES DIDN'T GET FAR into the empty building before he realized he'd set off the trap. The room shifted from shades of gray and blue to red and orange. The bare walls he'd seen from outside the door where now covered in symbols drawn in blood. Demon wraiths flew out of the broken bottles that covered the floor, freed from the voodoo totems that were lined up along the wall like sentinels. The spirits swirled around him like flames enveloping a witch being burned at the stake.

"Kendell, if you can hear me, do not come in here. It's a trap."

The sound of his voice set off the evil minions. They dove on him like piranhas devouring a carcass, but it wasn't his flesh they were after. His thoughts and memories became disjointed like a book having its pages ripped out and tossed into the wind.

"We meet again." The sound of the man's voice quieted the spirits of flame.

Myles found he couldn't move—not his legs, arms, or

even his eyes. His thoughts, however, could still form. *Who the hell are you?*

"I'm hurt. You don't recognize me? I suppose I was more spirit to your physical body last time. Now I'm the reality, and you're the interloper." Colin Malveaux walked around to face Myles.

He leaned on a metal rod. The top had been mangled into a handle. His clothing was impeccable, much like the loas of the dead but clean and better fitting. A scar snaked out from under the center of his top hat, ran along his forehead, and ended at his right eye.

You've looked better. Myles's defiance was one of the few things that had kept him sane while under Baron Malveaux's possession.

"Trust me, I've looked worse. When the old swamp bitch dropped me off here, I was barely a shadow of the man standing in front of you, but I've had time to learn about my environment. You and your friends were fools to challenge me in my own reality. Wicca may provide the bars to my prison cell, but I get to do whatever I want with the interior."

Without the wraiths chewing on his soul, Myles began to regain some functionality of his body. "Where am I? We can't have left your demon dimension, so I should have seen it from outside the door."

Colin swung the iron rod as he talked. Each time it hit the floor, sparks flew up as if he were poking a fire. "My dear daughter gave me the clues to building this cell. She explained I was in a school hallway. Such places are lined with lockers. This realm may only exist within the four walls of this room, but it is all mine."

Myles knew that the man, or rather the various men he used to be, never did anything impulsively. To have built this trap meant he wanted to capture a hostage. "What do you want?"

"I should think that would be obvious. I want to take this elevated being I've become and return to the land of the living, where I can be a god, though I'd settle for a devil—either one, really, so long as there are people to follow me."

The fact that neither Myles nor anyone of his group could give Colin what he wanted gave Myles a sense of peace. "We wouldn't give you what you wanted even if we could. So you might as well turn loose your demons to do their worst."

Colin moved his hand down to the shaft of his cane and slowly rotated the iron bar. Myles's body followed suit until he was facing the open door. Kendell stood at the entrance, horror stricken. "She can see you but not hear you. With my little pets dancing around your body, she can see the parts of your soul being chewed on like rats ripping at a block of cheese. Not a bad metaphor actually. You always were about as smart as curdled milk."

Myles closed his eyes to focus his attention on Kendell's soul. *You can hear me. I'm okay. He's only trying to scare you. Find the others, and get to work.*

He could feel her nod of understanding. When he opened his eyes, she was gone. "What, exactly, do you think is going to happen here?"

Myles watched the room spin as Colin turned him back

around. "Right about now, I expect Kendell is running to find Baron Samedi. I know you two opened the door. I should thank you for that, but after my first week or two here, I realized that wasn't the gate I was looking to open. A spirit like his out of his realm of power is kind of like a cartoon character come to life. They can make you laugh with their antics, but they can't really do anything of value."

At least keeping the devil talking worked as a distraction from him following Kendell. "Then why would you want her to run to Baron Samedi if he can't get you what you want?"

"All stepping stones along the path."

8

*K*endell ran down the streets of the Quarter in the dark, dodging the water-filled potholes. At least there weren't the drunk gutter punks to avoid. As she rounded Royal Street for the shortcut toward the Scratchy Dog, she plowed into Sanguine, who was running toward her.

"He's trapped the band. I didn't even see the voodoo dolls until Polly smashed the front window," Sanguine said between breathes.

"Apparently, Scratch and Sniff wasn't his only snare. He's got Myles too. We need the cane, and we need it now. But all I've got is Samedi's vague description of it not being in this reality and the fact that Colin already stole it from Marie's tomb."

"If Colin didn't have it with him, where would he hide it?"

"It has to be in his office. If Myles can keep him

distracted long enough, we should be able to sneak in and steal it."

Sanguine took Kendell's arm, not letting her start down the street toward the high-rise. "Then what? Once again, you need to think beyond the next obvious step. So what if we have the cane?"

Sometimes acting fast was better than sitting around talking. "It's the first step. Once we have it, we can figure out how to stick the silver skull back on. Then I'll beat him over the head with it if I have to. Who cares what we do next? We've got to seize this opportunity while we can."

Kendell pulled her arm out of Sanguine's grasp and started running through the Quarter. If they had to strategize, they could at least keep moving while they did so. From behind her, Sanguine kept offering up obstacles like garbage tossed into the road. "So you're just going to fix the cane like he wants—again. My grandmother isn't going to whip up another hurricane to save us this time."

"Once we have the cane, we can get Baron Samedi out of his cage."

"Please don't tell me you're looking for some big, strong voodoo lord to save you. I've never imagined you to be the submissive type of woman."

Kendell nearly stopped to confront Sanguine. "If we didn't have to get this thing before Colin loses interest in torturing Myles, I'd be more than happy to explain to you how I am *not* looking for a man to save me. But sometimes people, and spirits, have their uses."

The towering office building didn't look all that

different from the last time Kendell had confronted Colin, then known as Lincoln Laroque, in his penthouse office.

"You're not worried that this is another trap?" Sanguine asked.

Kendell had been considering the possibility for the last two blocks. "It's possible, but Delphine didn't have an unlimited number of voodoo totems. So far, that seems to be the extent of Colin's powers—using what someone else created. You can stay out here if you think it'd be safer."

"No. I'm not going to be the last woman standing in hell. Of the two of us, you're the stronger."

Kendell turned away from the glass entry doors and back toward Sanguine. "I think that's the first compliment you've ever given me."

"You mean more to me than any sister ever could, but that also involves you having to deal with my snarkiness."

"Fair enough," Kendell said. "At the risk of you calling me stupid again, do we just walk in? It's not like he'd have any guards."

Sanguine picked up a rock that formed part of the landscaping border and threw it like a baseball pitcher at the glass door. The barrier shattered, covering the marble entry floor with miniature glass pebbles. "How's that for stupid?"

After twenty-seven years of conditioning, Kendell expected some kind of alarm or armed security officer. "You've proven we can break in, but just in case there's some kind of paranormal alarm system, we'd better get moving." Even with the lack of armed response, Kendell avoided the elevator. "It's a long way up, but my gullibility only goes so far."

"Agreed. I'm never averse to a little physical exercise."

Kendell consulted the wall directory. "Climbing fifty-five stories isn't what I consider a light workout, but if you can do it, so can I."

Sanguine bolted for the door. "Last one to the top is a Hogwarts dropout."

By the fifth floor, Kendell was sorry she'd inadvertently caused Sanguine to challenge her. Buy the twentieth, she no longer knew how much higher her friend was up the stairwell.

"Come on, slowpoke." The younger woman's words echoed down the shaft.

"Now, *this* is stupid." But Kendell knew Sanguine couldn't have heard her.

Sports had never been Kendell's passion in school. It wasn't the physical exertion. She had plenty of boyfriends who would attest to her stamina. It was the damn uniforms. She focused on her irritation at the school system's inability to make exercise a lifelong activity, and her anger made the next twenty floors much easier to climb.

By the forty-seventh floor, she caught Sanguine gasping for air on the landing. "This is a marathon, not a sprint."

"Suddenly, the idea of taking the elevator doesn't seem so foolish," Sanguine said. "You don't suppose we could just jump out the window to go back down, do you?"

Laughing hurt Kendell's sides. "Maybe. After all, this reality is nothing more than your grandmother's imagination. Come on. We're almost there."

They climbed the remaining steps together. "No more stairs. I guess this must be the place."

Kendell pushed on the release bar across the door. "He didn't even lock it. What do you suppose that means?"

"If we're lucky, it means he didn't think anyone would be dumb enough to walk up fifty-five flights of stairs."

Kendell wasn't sure if it was the exhaustion or her time hanging out with Sanguine, but she was beginning to see the worst-case scenarios all around her. "It could be a trap. He's just sadistic enough to wait until we'd done all that work before springing it on us."

"Very good. But I suspect it's more likely that he wants us to find the cane. If I were in danger, my grandmother would let me know. Come on. I didn't come all this way to turn around now." Sanguine pushed past Kendell into the room walled with windows. "For a jailbird, this is one impressive perch."

Kendell almost wished the cane had been locked up somewhere. "He just left it on his desk? That's kind of insulting."

"Right? Even if he did want us to find the cane, the least he could have done was let us ransack his office. Think there's anything else in here worth stealing? I'm not in the mood to just pick this up and head back down those stairs. Though maybe that's his way of torturing us."

The office had only the most basic furnishings, but from the rumpled look of the sofa cushions, Kendell guessed this was where Colin spent the bulk of his time. She opened a small cabinet. "Look at this. He's been a busy inmate. These

89

pages look like a rundown of his hell. Maybe he's done the work for us."

"Or he's figured out another way to trick us."

Kendell divided the pile in half. "We'll go through what he knows then verify it when we're back out on the street."

"Why not just take the pages and run? He's going to know we were here when he doesn't see the cane on his desk."

Kendell looked out the window toward the Quarter. "True. And time is against us. But if we don't steal them, he won't know what we know. He would expect we were here just for the cane."

"Okay, but let's take turns watching for his return. I don't want to get trapped in here."

Kendell scanned the pile on her lap. If they didn't have much time, she didn't want to miss anything important. "This first section looks to be his attempts at interpreting Marie's journals. Most of this stuff I already know, or he got wrong." Being careful to remember the order of the pages, she turned the first batch over and started again. "Observations of his surroundings. He could have at least titled what he was writing. Stream-of-consciousness ramblings aren't helpful to anyone."

Sanguine handed over the pages she'd been looking at. "Maybe you'll find this more interesting."

Kendell started making notes like mad. Colin hadn't so much figured out how his world worked scientifically as built a religion based on his findings. Unfortunately for him, he hadn't had Delphine as a teacher to explain the inner workings of voodoo.

"Time to go. I see him coming down the street."

"One last thing to do." Kendell pulled out the golden pick from Papa Ghede and put it in her palm.

"What are you doing? We need to get out of here."

The triangle turned in her hand. "Baron Samedi said the cane would have its own energy, different from anything else here. I'm betting there's another object that might have that same signature. If I'm right, this little goodie from Guinee might point the way."

She felt the pick struggle toward a spot in the middle of the floor. But as she leaned down and touched the floor, all she felt was the solid marble tile. "Nothing."

"Too bad. Let's go. He's nearly at the front door."

"It's here, I just can't touch it. I think it fell through the floor."

Sanguine started moving toward the stairs. "Kendell, we don't have time for this. Remember what I said about my grandmother giving me a heads-up if there's danger? Based on my adrenaline level, I think she's shouting in my ear."

The golden pick grew heavier in Kendell's hand. "You want to go down there?"

"Yes, I'd like to get the fuck out of here."

She looked up at Sanguine. "Not you, the pick." She dropped it on the floor. Like a magnet, it slid to the halfway point of the white tile with gray streaks. She had trouble working her fingernails under the edges. "I think it's got a hold of something. Give me a hand."

"If it gets you out of here any faster, I'll give you Marie Laveau's hand."

Kendell squeezed the fingernails of both hands under

the pick like a human steam shovel. "Pull on my arms. Help me lift this thing."

With Sanguine's help, Kendell got the pick off the floor. The wooden head that followed it out of the tile made Sanguine scream and nearly let go of her arms. "What the hell is that thing?"

"It's the voodoo totem that Delphine used to capture Baron Malveaux once he was exorcised from Myles."

"I don't remember Colin writing anything about a creepy wooden head being hidden in his floor."

Kendell kept hold of the pick and turned the sculpture toward her. "I'm betting he didn't know about it. See here? This is where the glass spirit jar is supposed to be. I'll bet he smashed it once he swallowed the baron Malveaux's energy."

"What the hell do you want it for?"

"It's not something that belongs in this world," Kendell said. "I'm betting it will work like a wooden barrel some fool would use to go over Niagara Falls. Only this one would take a soul from this realm back to Guinee."

"We'll have to fix it first. Know of any voodoo totem repairmen? Because I'm guessing they're pretty scarce even among the living."

"You always need to know the answers. Sometimes you've gotta take what weapons you can find and figure out how to use them later." The bell from the elevator made Kendell jump to her feet. "*Now* it's time to go. We'll need to be as quiet as possible going down the stairs."

With the pick firmly implanted between the wooden head's square nailheads, Kendell was able to handle the relic while Sanguine held the cane via Maria Laveau's bones as they descended.

Out on the street, Kendell breathed a little easier. "See, that wasn't so bad."

"Now that we have your voodoo tchotchkes, which way do we go?"

Kendell nodded toward the tall Romanesque building in the Quarter. "First I'm going to drop these off with Baron Samedi, then I need to free the band. You're the most in tune with this realm, so you should probably work with Samedi to figure out what we can do with these voodoo items in this Wiccan reality."

"What about Myles?"

"The band first. We're going to need them," Kendell said, though she hated leaving her boyfriend in any more distress than absolutely necessary.

"How did you know that thing was in his office, anyway?"

"It was something you said about your grandmother— that she would warn you if you were in danger. We've been acting like this is a level playing field. It isn't. We have the advantage. It's time we started using it. He might have a better understanding of how things work here, but for each attempt he makes at magic, it will ultimately obey us."

9

With Colin gone, his demon horde once again dove at Myles's soul. Like a demented version of catch and release, they ripped out mouthfuls of his essence then spit them back into place. He felt like a shattered window that didn't have the good sense to explode.

In self-defense, he retreated toward the *deep waters*, but instead of finding the peace of all of humanity, he hit hell's brick wall. His senses were reduced to transmitted messages without the expectation of a response. The room smelled of sulfur and scalded soul. The sounds of the wraiths reminded him of greatly amplified fingernails on a chalkboard. Ash and charcoal coated his mouth like a sticky paste he couldn't spit out. Every nerve ending fired off its electrical shocks of pain. But when he saw the black creature standing in the doorway, he knew he was in real trouble.

The wraiths were nothing more than disembodied spirits. They could set off his senses and tear at his soul, but they were tormentors only, not a true physical threat. But apparently, they weren't the only demonic creatures in Colin's hell. The animal that crept slowly into the room glared at him with glowing red eyes. Saliva dripped from its open mouth. Teeth that resembled sharpened ivory daggers interlocked then separated to reveal the creature's black tongue and cavernous mouth.

The hell apparition lunged at Myles with the speed of a giant cat and the ferocity of a grizzly bear. But instead of ripping off one of Myles's appendages, it circled around him, snarling at every wraith. A line of fur extended up from between the creature's eyes, running along the top of its head and down its back and ending at the tip of its tail.

The band of demons backed away from Myles and the circling creature. He began to catch his breath from the torture. The creature stood at attention at his side until the flaming specters settled down from bright yellow to dull red.

The animal turned its attention to Myles and let out three blood-curdling barks.

Myles stared intently at the dark red eyes. "Doughnut Hole?"

The animal gave him a big, terror-inducing smile.

One of the wraiths misinterpreted the show of recognition for weakness. It dove at Myles. The puppy-turned-hellhound sprung to his feet and intercepted the creature of fire in midflight. Instead of passing through the incorporeal demon, Doughnut Hole ripped a huge section from the wraith's head.

The being's screeches of pain and surprise sent the other spirits into a panic. Like a sheepdog of the damned, Doughnut Hole cut a wraith from the horde and sent it screeching back behind the voodoo totem it had come from. Any that had the audacity not to obey the hound found themselves losing a body part. The orange-and-blue liquid fire that gushed from the injured wraiths pooled on the floor.

Without the spirits circling him, Myles no longer found himself metaphorically tied to the stake. His muscles ached, but they worked. But with Doughnut Hole continuing his mission, Myles thought it best to remain where he stood.

Finally, every one of Colin's little pets cowered behind its voodoo doll cage. Doughnut Hole circled the room one more time, growling at every sculpture to drive his point home to the wraith hiding behind it.

He returned to Myles and sat at attention in front of him. Though the creature's appearance would cause the worst demon to run in fear, Myles could make out a smile of satisfaction.

"You are such a good boy. Let's go find the others."

Doughnut Hole gave him a playful yap, danced around in a circle the way his mother often did when happy, and led the way out the door.

Myles wondered what he must have looked like chasing after a hellhound down the darkened streets of the French Quarter. If there were any other demons, they kept their distance.

The cacophony from the Scratchy Dog filled Frenchmen Street from Royal to Decatur. Myles did his best to keep up with Doughnut Hole, but at the sound of his sisters snarling and yipping, the dog broke into a full run, and Myles fell behind.

∾

KENDELL'S HEART leapt in her chest at seeing Myles standing out front of the Scratchy Dog. Her joy turned to terror when she noticed the rabid animal that clearly had him cornered against the wall of the club. She picked up a brick and got ready to throw it. "Get away from him!"

Myles turned toward her and waved his hands downward. "Hush. Put that thing down. You don't want to spook them."

She lowered her hand, confused. "What the hell's going on?"

He smiled mischievously. "I didn't recognize him at first either. This is Doughnut Hole. His sisters are guarding the band. But two little puppies are no match for a room full of demons. My boy was able to get me out because it was just me. Apparently, the more people they have to feed on, the more powerful the wraiths become. Where's Sanguine?"

"She's with Baron Samedi, trying to figure out how to get Marie's hand off the cane." Even with his assurance, she chose to stand on his side, opposite the hellhound, and kept the brick in her hand. Inside the club, two similar creatures, but with the colored markings she remembered from the pups, circled the women in a clockwise direction while the flame demons circled counter-clockwise. Neither the dogs nor the wraiths were backing down. "What are we going to do? And if these are her pups, where's Cheesecake?"

"Even though we can hear the dogs, the women can't hear us, but I've been able to signal the band to keep calm. The wraiths get spun up when they sense fear. Colin said his traps were based on a slight variation to this dimension. We need a way to bridge this reality with the one the band's occupying."

Kendell surveyed the stage, where her bandmates were huddled. "Good. They've already got their equipment." She turned to the VW, which, as the only car in hell, occupied the prime front-of-club parking space. Her acoustic guitar was still propped against the back seat. She stayed low to avoid distracting the pups and rushed for the open sliding door. Her white instrument looked like a beacon of hope in the darkness.

She slung Cecile into place like a gunslinger at high noon and faced her band. Each woman gave a nod of understanding. Though they moved slowly so as not to break the demon puppies' circle of protection, each woman managed to retrieve an instrument. With Polly standing in the center like the leader that she was, the other three musicians huddled as close as their equipment would allow.

Kendell stared into Polly's eyes, willing her to know which song she would play. The lead singer watched Kendell's fingers as she strummed out the opening chords to Tom Petty's "I Won't Back Down."

It never took Polly long to pick up the beat. She nodded at Kendell and yelled something to the other band members before grabbing the microphone. But throughout the song, all Kendell could get from her girls was their shared energy and looks of concern.

"It didn't work. I thought for sure the music would bust down the invisible wall."

Doughnut Hole barked at his sisters, but they only gave him a passing glance as they maintained their vigil.

Myles put his hand on Kendell's back. "Try again. Even if it takes an entire set, you can break through."

When she looked back at her band, she saw Lynn trying to get her attention. With exaggerated movements, Lynn hammered out "Break on Through," by the Doors. By the end of the song, Kendell could feel cracks forming in the demons' resistance.

Doughnut Hole danced like a dog who'd seen the stick thrown but had been told to hold his stance.

Scraper pushed Polly aside and began slapping her bass to "Personal Jesus."

Knowing her shaved-head bandmate was more into original music than remakes, even if the remake was by Johnny Cash, Kendell went into the Depeche Mode version of the song.

As the number faded out, Kendell picked up on what the band had already figured out: each needed to establish her own way home. She turned to Minerva to see which song the drummer would pick.

Instead of busting into a song, though, Minerva turned to her fellow member of the percussion section. Scraper nodded and turned to Kendell and pulled on her earlobe to expose the golden earring.

Kendell nodded and laid down the opening riff to "Radar Love." As Polly sang about a love coming in from above, a hole in the ghostly apparitions appeared along the floor. Doughnut Hole dove into the opening as if it were a doggy door into hell.

Kendell kept playing, but watching the demon dog team up with his sisters made her worry once again for everyone in the club. Doughnut Hole wasn't simply going to protect the women from the demons. His snarl and lunging made it clear he intended to do battle.

She spoke to Myles without yelling over the song. "He's going to get himself hurt."

"He's his mama's son. Don't worry. That little guy has hell smarts."

Sure enough, the wraiths lost their cohesive show of strength. The two girl hellhounds deferred to their brother. The first flame spirit they encountered rose up like an inferno, but Doughnut Hole wasn't allowing the show of bluster. Kendell watched in horror as he launched off his haunches straight into the middle of the beast. Flames erupted around the room like a firework that had gone off without getting airborne.

Kendell couldn't take it any longer. She pulled off her guitar and started for the door. Before she could get there, the two female hellhounds nearly knocked her over. They were quickly followed by the four band members. Once the women were safely outside, Kendell held them all close. But Doughnut Hole hadn't made his escape.

She turned back to the inferno that filled the room,

fearful she'd see the puppy engaged in a battle for his sweet young life.

Myles put his arm around her waist. "Watch this. That little guy has got mad skills when it comes to wrangling demons."

One by one, Doughnut Hole corralled the wraiths back to their voodoo totems. Each one lost so much energy that it was little more than a lit candle compared to the raging bonfire it had been while attacking the band members.

"We're going to need to find a supply of hellhound-puppy treats. Some spirit bottles to contain the demons Colin freed would be useful too."

Myles didn't let her go. "I don't want to worry you, but Cheesecake is still missing."

She hadn't forgotten about the most important member of the pack. "If she was in trouble, her puppies would be racing after her. And I'd know."

COLIN HAD EXPECTED some move by Kendell, but as he stared at his desk where the bony arm and incorporeal cane were supposed to be, he realized he'd misjudged her. "That must have been quite the climb, little witch. Even if I didn't have the only set of keys to the elevator, the energy in this building…"

Something had changed. He grabbed his notes out of the alcohol cupboard. "This is my domain. The energy the old swamp witch used to create it was based on my life."

He knew it wasn't that simple. Being made up of two

spirits meant the witch had her pick of souls to use for different areas of his prison, but his office had always been as comfortable as old shoes. Now it felt like stiff leather that chafed his feet.

"What did you do?" As far as he could tell, nothing other than the missing witch bones and cane had been removed.

Every part of his being screamed that he was no longer completely in charge. He needed answers. Confronting Kendell again didn't seem the best way to get them, even if he did have her band and boyfriend imprisoned. "That little girl is really getting on my nerves."

He headed down to the lobby, wondering where he should start. The cold steel of his improvised walking cane reminded him how far he'd come. When time still mattered to him, he'd spent days focusing on the smallest tear to his shirt until he could see the individual broken threads. By pouring his energy into the break, he found the small tendrils could be coaxed back together by force of will. That tear in his shirt had been the hardest learning experience of his life. Once he'd accomplished that simple mind repair, however, the rest of his environment started obeying his commands like an attack dog that just needed to know who was boss.

Walking still involved leaning heavily on the mangled iron rod. His bones didn't enjoy the same pliability as the cage he lived in. He could bend metal in his mental forges and bash it into shape with pile drivers but couldn't fix his own living flesh.

The night air helped bring him out of his funk. He'd turned one of the most fearsome aspects of his incarceration into a blessing. "I may not be a vampire, but I am a creature of the night. Perpetual darkness is paradise."

One by one, he'd faced his fears of hell and overcome each to the point that his environment respected him as its god. Turning loose the demons Delphine kept so cruelly isolated in their wooden sculptures had given him the army he'd desired and completed his mastery of hell.

Analyzing his rise to power only made the new feeling of weakness more infuriating. Without realizing it, he started walking toward the bank, stomping his cane hard against the brick sidewalk with every stride. He'd face the one adversary he truly understood, Baron Samedi. Though he'd had help in stealing the cane originally and had Baron Kriminel to thank for his position in Guinee, the fact remained that he'd bested one of the greatest loas of the dead. Even if the weakened spirit didn't have answers, going up against him again would feel good. At the moment, that would be enough.

Colin only made it to the top step of the bank. Standing in the open doorway was the hated voodoo totem that had held him prisoner. The square-cut nails that covered the top of the wooden sculpture made his hair bristle. He squinted in hatred at the sewn-shut leather eyelids, mouth, and ears. "You no longer contain me."

A snarl from behind him made him swing around. A four-foot-tall she-wolf crept menacingly up the marble steps. Her black-and-white markings blended so well into the shadows he wasn't sure if she were animal or specter.

He raised his metal cane. "Back off. I'm the devil here,

and you're just a simple hell beast. You are under my command."

But the creature continued to snarl and move closer. He could bash her with his cane, but he'd only get one shot. With his damaged leg, he was no match for an attack dog the size of a small bear. As he backed toward the bank entrance, he felt the pull of the voodoo totem. His soul was weakening.

"So that's your play. Corner me, and you'll see exactly what lengths I'll go to in defending my position. Who's commanding you?"

"I just wanted you to see that your reality can be much worse than you imagine."

He recognized the woman's voice even though he'd only met her once. Colin aimed his cane at the she-wolf and half turned toward the young swamp witch standing inside the bank. "You. I should have known. That little witch and her idiot boyfriend wouldn't have the imagination to confront me, but as the old swamp witch bat's granddaughter, you feel right at home here. Call off your dog."

"She's not my dog. Honestly, I don't even know what she's doing here. All I wanted to do was frighten you with this little rodent trap. Between Kendell and Baron Samedi, we figured out how to open it again. It would appear this hell has its own breed of animal protectors."

He'd investigated his surroundings enough to know animals weren't uncommon, but the largest he'd run into in the city were the nutria river rats. The wolf circled around to the top of the stairs and took up an attack stance next to

Sanguine. The red eyes and sharp white teeth made it clear the animal was looking for an excuse to attack.

"Hello, girl." Baron Samedi stepped out of the shadows and rubbed the evil incarnation's rear haunches.

Instead of ripping the loa's arm out by its socket, the she-wolf gave up her attack stance and wagged her tail at the greeting.

"So she's yours. I had no idea loas of the dead kept pets." Colin didn't like surprises, especially not in his realm.

"I wouldn't want to ruin the revelation for you. There's so little about this world that astonishes anymore. I think if you check on your little flame children, you'll find this creature has more power than you suspect. Now, run along and play. You're no longer welcome at the seventh gate."

As he walked away from the bank, Colin couldn't remember the last time someone had sent him packing. Though he could justify the encounter as a standoff, he had to admit that he'd lost. They hadn't taken anything from him, and his situation hadn't changed from when he'd walked out of his office. Still, for the first time, he was at a strategic disadvantage.

He didn't so much fear what he'd see in Delphine's shop as grow determined to let out his anger should his demons have failed in their task of tormenting Myles. It took a true sadist to continually find new areas of weakness in his victims while keeping them conscious and alive. In all likelihood, the she-wolf had ripped the bartender to shreds at seeing his vulnerability. Still, Colin's wraiths should have found a way to stop her. Their job wasn't simply to play with the fool.

"Oh well. Even if he is dead, I'll find some other way to influence that little witchy girl. I do still have her bandmates." The four women who made up the band that gave the little guitarist's life meaning had to be more important than a lovey-dovey romantic partner.

He stood stock-still in the doorway to Scratch and Sniff. "You let him escape!" Every blood cell in his body felt as if it were about to boil.

His attention progressed from the bare wood floor to the glowing totems along the walls. "For the love of hell. You are demon wraiths, not fireflies. One little doggy comes into your dungeon, and you lose all your intensity?"

He'd only spent a few months trapped in the voodoo totem and then had been released into another human being. The demons that huddled behind their wooden entrapments had been incarcerated for so long the spells used weren't even known any longer. They'd become the proverbial prisoners who'd served so many years they refused to leave when freed.

Though he understood the syndrome, he had no patience for his demons.

10

The excitement of having freed her band, combined with having Myles at her side, drove Kendell to want to search for Cheesecake. "She wouldn't have sent her puppies over here alone. There are only a couple of places she could be."

Myles pointed down Frenchmen Street. "Like escorting Sanguine back to the band?"

Though others had described Cheesecake-the-she-wolf to Kendell, in every other realm, all she'd seen was her precious pup. The intimidating animal that walked at Sanguine's side could have been any number of mythical beasts.

As the creature broke into a run, Kendell saw the love in the dog's eyes. The embrace knocked her to the ground. "Easy, girl. You're bigger than you think."

The three much smaller and leaner hellhounds yipped for joy at seeing their mother return to the pack.

Cheesecake gave Kendell one last kiss before turning to her brood. Their play reminded Kendell of the small dogs having so much fun on the other side of the river. In their hell-demon personas they looked as if they were devouring some animal three times their size.

Sanguine helped Kendell to her feet. "She did good. Honestly, I didn't even know it was Cheesecake until she started pulling on my shirt to follow her."

Though Kendell was relieved to see her pup safe and sound, there was still work to do. "Did Baron Samedi have any luck with the cane?"

"No. With that golden pick of yours, he was able to open the voodoo totem. Scared the shit out of Colin, or rather the Malveaux side of him. I guess being locked in complete blackness wasn't enjoyable for him. Cheesecake nearly made him wet his pants when she started forcing him toward the doll."

Myles couldn't take five steps without Doughnut Hole coming to his side. "The same happened when Hell Hole saved me. The wraiths were none too happy about returning to their cages."

Kendell looked over at her bandmates who, though still hesitant to approach the animals, were giving warm words of praise to the frightening hellhounds. "We have some definite advantages, but all we've accomplished is getting the cane from Colin. It still doesn't work in this realm. The walls of this jail are still weak, and Samedi is still trapped."

Sanguine kicked at the curb. The little-girl act made Kendell suspect she wasn't going to like what the young swamp witch was about to report. "I'm afraid Samedi wasn't very helpful when it came to his cane. He agreed we need to stick the silver skull back on, but he didn't know anything about the spell Marie Laveau cast."

Kendell nodded. "Delphine knew at some point we'd need to contact the land of the living. We couldn't risk having Marie's diary and the cane both in this realm. She said we'd need to find the portal from hell to life. We know the seventh gate is the door from hell to Guinee, so that's not it."

Sanguine cocked her head to the side as if an idea needed to roll down her brain to in front of her eyes. "I read something in Colin's office. He met a version of his daughter, Serephine, in the Laurette mansion."

Kendell stared hard at the girl. "You didn't think that was important?"

She shrugged. "You were getting all hot and bothered about digging that totem out of the marble floor. I didn't think we had time to discuss our findings."

Kendell turned to Myles. "As the first victim, Serephine would be connected to the curse. She might be willing to help. Though it's not *our* reality, at least it might be a place to start."

He rubbed at the stubble on his chin. "She was the first victim, but her brother was the first to stand guard against their father's evil. Even though she was the one to talk to Colin, maybe it was Antoine who opened the door. Either way, the Laurette mansion seems like the most obvious portal."

Sanguine leaned against the side of the van and bit her lip. "To remove the skull, we needed Delphine de Galpion to read from Marie's journal while Kendell and I perform our magic. I'd guess putting it back on will also require the three of us."

Kendell remembered all too well how Colin had sat in the living room like a despot expecting to be crowned king while they tried to power up his scepter like a bunch of mystical nymphs. "Going to the mansion would only alert Colin, and taking the cane and skull to the house seems like a good way to lose it all to our adversary. Maybe if we free Samedi, he could zap it over to her or something."

Sanguine shook her head. "No go. The one thing he did say was Marie's bones are holding the cane to this reality. Its powers may not work here, and we can't grab it, but she's preventing Baron Samedi from taking it as well."

"Peachy," Kendell said. "Anything else you think isn't important?"

"You asked if we made any progress. We didn't. Don't get mad at me just because I answered your questions."

"Enough," Myles said. "Sanguine, take everyone and the silver skull back to the bank. It's the one place we know is safe. Kendell and I will figure out how to contact Delphine. We need to know what we're doing before we go off half-cocked."

Cheesecake sat at Kendell's side as the women loaded into the VW for the short ride. The puppies looked from their mother to the bus. She jutted her snout toward the van and gave them a firm bark. Muffin Top and Cupcake quickly obliged and climbed into the vehicle, but Doughnut Hole lay on the ground, whimpering, as he looked from Cheesecake to Myles.

Though it was Cheesecake's place to direct her unruly son, Myles walked over to the reluctant hellhound and knelt down to his level. "I'll be okay, boy. Go protect the women."

Cheesecake let out a much more definitive bark, one that said she meant business. The pup got up and slinked to the open van door.

The scene tugged at Kendell's heart. "In case you missed it, that dog has chosen you as his human. I recognize the signs. Cheesecake was the same way when we first met. She wouldn't leave my side."

"I just hope our apartment will allow two dogs."

It warmed Kendell's heart knowing Doughnut Hole would be permanently joining their little family. "Now, how do we contact Antoine? I suppose we could ransack the Laurette mansion, looking for some Civil War item hidden in what's left of the walls."

Myles had the worried look he often got when considering an idea she wouldn't like. "I'm not connected to the *deep waters*, so taking a psychometric trip won't work. We need a more direct connection—something Antoine would respond to without being called from the beyond."

Kendell remembered every item they'd found while investigating Fleurentine Malveaux's trunks. "We have to go to Minerva's garage in the Bywater."

Cheesecake trotted along beside them as they strolled through the Marigny to the Bywater like a couple of tourists out to see the historic yet bohemian neighborhood. The old shotgun double painted in bright shades of blue, yellow, and purple didn't quite look complete without the VW bus parked out back.

Kendell found the key hidden under the drain pipe and worked the uneven garage door off the ground. Its hinges creaked as though they didn't have many more openings left in them.

Myles gave the neighborhood one good look before joining her in the cluttered storage space. "I guess the bus doesn't spend much time in here."

She pointed to the door, which hung at an angle on its hinges. "It wouldn't fit through there. Give me a hand moving some of these boxes. I told Minerva to bury Fleurentine Malveaux's trunks in case anyone was looking for them. Apparently, she took me a little more literally than I expected."

The heavy steamer trunks weren't hard to distinguish from the cardboard boxes and suitcases, but Kendell and Myles had to pull four of the five out before she found the trunk filled with old gowns.

"I stashed her keepsakes at the bottom of this one." Kendell pulled out a worn leather memory album and turned to the last page. "I thought this was creepy as hell when I first saw it—enough so that I did a little investigating. Art made from the hair of loved ones was still popular during the Civil War." Carefully, she removed the wire-frame flower covered in shades of blond hair.

"I've heard of mothers keeping locks of their infants' hair, but nothing like this."

She turned it slowly in the dim light. "It's not just from Antoine as a child. People used to collect hair over a person's lifetime. See how only the center is soft and how it gets bristlier and darker as the petals move outward?"

From Myles's expression, she could tell that he felt the way she first had—a combination of curious and disgusted. "You've made your point. If Antoine's going to respond to anything, it'd be a piece of art made by his mother out of his own hair."

"Now that we have the item, how do we call him?"

He took the small three-dimensional flower and turned it slowly. "I can't access the *deep waters*, but I am getting enough of an emotional reading to think I can contact him directly. We can try my usual approach and see what happens. So long as it's just Antoine we're trying to reach, Colin shouldn't be able to butt in."

She grabbed an old army duffle bag covered in travel patches. "This belonged to Minerva's grandfather. We found it stashed behind the seats when we cleaned out the VW. He used to do a lot of traveling."

Down feathers erupted from the canvas sack as she pulled out a moth-eaten sleeping bag. "This should at least keep us off the wet concrete."

"So long as the old dude didn't have too many adventures in that thing," Myles joked. "I'd hate to end up watching Minerva's grandparents getting it on at some free-love commune."

"We'll just be a couple of hippies lying under the stars, contemplating our flower."

Once in position, Myles gave her his usual list of warnings. "I don't know what's going to happen. We're not in our reality with time moving forward. I've only done this when I knew how to get back to my body."

She hugged his arm tightly to her side. "We'll be

together. You'll get us home. And I have Cheesecake to focus on."

She did her best to mirror his ritual of letting go of his life one aspect at a time until they were pure spirits without memories, names, or bodies. Kendell hadn't reached the soul-bonding closeness with Myles when she heard a man's voice coming from the open garage door. "So you've found me. What do you want?"

She looked at Myles in confusion. Other trips they'd taken had been purely mental, but this time, every sensation of her body—down to the prickly thorns in her back from some long-dead weed that the sleeping bag had covered— was as clear as when she'd lain down.

Antoine seemed to understand her confusion. "Think of our connections to that hair like the old-fashioned child's game of telephone—two tin cans and a string. Only instead of traversing a distance, it's across dimensions."

Myles sat up. "So you're the gatekeeper between life and hell?"

The man half turned toward the night sky. His profile reminded Kendell of an old daguerreotype of a former Civil War soldier. Moonlight filtered through his long wiry beard. Lines were etched in his face. The sorrow in his eyes struck deep into her soul.

"My father believed in voodoo. His fascination with it led to the curse. As you might imagine, such a pursuit didn't hold any appeal for me. However, I saw enough during the war to know there was more to reality than life and death. I was an old man when I met Agnes Delarosa. She promised me a way of containing not just my father's spirit but also the evil he'd created. I have to say, I expected better."

Kendell felt bad for the old man. He'd spent his life trying to protect his family from the curse and never had the resources to combat the man who'd caused it. "We have Baron Samedi's cane and the silver skull that controls its power, but we need to figure out how to connect the two. Once we can use its magic, we can help you."

"Voodoo again." Antoine sighed. "You'll need to talk to Delphine de Galpion. I'll open a portal."

The back of the Bywater double faded to black, and then a projection of Scratch and Sniff's back room filled the garage opening. Delphine walked into the voodoo library and sat at her African-motif throne. "I'm ready." She closed her eyes.

The window into life made Kendell's heart ache, but she didn't have time for such emotions. "What is the significance of Marie Laveau holding the cane? Do I sing to it to get her to let go?"

Delphine talked in the monotone she used when in a trance. "She wrote that only the one who was meant to have the cane would be able to make her let it go. Like Colin, I assumed she meant during her life—that she'd stolen it from Guinee for a specific person. Of course, the obvious answer was Archibald Malveaux, but from what Baron Samedi and Papa Ghede said about him taking it from Marie, I'm no longer sure about that interpretation. If her specter now holds the cane, I'm guessing the rightful heir hasn't come forward yet. So long as she's in possession of the cane, she'll have a say in how it's used—even if it's just her bony dead hand that's holding it."

Kendell felt relief that Delphine had found a way of keeping track of what was happening in hell. She filed the information away for a later time. "Baron Samedi said once we affix it to this hell, he can work with it, but what if the bones aren't removed?"

"The loas know everything, and I'm just a student, but they aren't always to be trusted. Their perception of time, space, and reality differs so much from what we endure that it's hard to know when they're helping and when they're not. Making the cane real in your current situation seems like a good move so long as Colin doesn't end up with it. Just be careful."

Kendell pulled out a piece of paper from her pocket and started taking notes. "Right. How do we do that?"

11

*C*heesecake's pups were standing guard at the bank entrance. In spite of their ferocious appearance, Kendell desperately wanted to give each one a giant hug, but there was work to do and an enemy possibly watching from the shadows. Colin would gain too much power if he realized the fearsome beasts who'd gotten the better of him were actually Kendell's sweet girl and her pups.

The she-wolf took up position with the other guard dogs as Kendell entered the bank. A quick wag of the tail told her that Cheesecake was also aware of the situation. "You dogs all deserve special treats when we get back."

Doughnut Hole let out a quiet whimper as Myles patted his head, but he remained at his post.

Kendell snuggled close to Myles's side as they faced the band, Sanguine, and Baron Samedi. "We have a plan," she said. "It'll take all of us to pull it off, but Delphine is confident if we perform the ritual to the letter, the silver skull will connect to the cane. Sanguine, as you're Wiccan and not part of the voodoo tradition, all Delphine could say was you needed to provide some form of energy and would know what would work."

Sanguine, usually the first to show reservation about one of Kendell's ideas, was surprisingly upbeat. "The plants around here won't do me any good, but dance has often proved a powerful means of casting spells."

Kendell consulted the pages of sheet music. "That actually might work better than you think. Baron Samedi, the cane once belonged to you. Your blessing is needed to make this work."

The thin man behind the desk had grown so ghostly pale she wasn't sure if he was even still part of this astral plane. "I'll hold the cane during the ceremony. That should pacify any deity that might question my approval."

She wondered if he'd be capable of anything other than sitting behind the desk with the cane in hand. The band was going to be the hard part. As she handed out the sheet music, she hoped each member would take a breath before responding.

"No. Are you kidding?" Polly usually took point on any issue on which she had an even passing opinion.

Kendell leaned back against the oversized wooden desk in the elegant bank office. "It has to be this one."

Lynn usually tried to find a compromise everyone could live with. "I get the idea, but couldn't we go with 'Twist and Shout' or even 'Twistin' the Night Away'? It just seems like this is a little not us."

Scraper said, "This should be the theme song for the

Mutants at Table Nine. In fact, I think I've heard them play it."

Kendell had to rein in the situation. "The cane isn't some twist-top Coke bottle. The skull has to be firmly spun on. For this to work across dimensions, Delphine needs to be singing the same song as we are. This is the only number she knows that will work for us. The woman is not musically inclined."

Minerva kept staring at the page as though she expected to see a different song. "This song was cheesy when it came out. It's the opposite of punk—more like puke."

Baron Samedi toyed with the cane by holding the femur and twirling it like a propeller. "So none of you wishes to play the number? Perfect. Remember, this is hell. Once you play the piece, you won't want to ever do it again. We're casting a spell here, not entertaining an audience. Without knowing the piece, based on the strong emotional reaction each of you is giving off, I'd have to guess it will continue in humanity's awareness—what you call *history*. That's also helpful in maintaining the connection."

Polly gave the page another once-over. "Well, I can't sing it. It was meant for a man's voice."

Minerva handed her a tambourine. "Join me and Scraper in the rhythm section. We're going to need all the help we can get to keep this thing on track."

Kendell knew she had to get going with casting the spell before she faced a full revolt. "I'll do the singing. Lynn, care to start us off?"

"Only under duress, *baby*."

"Well, you do *look like you're lots of fun*," Polly joked.

By the time the chorus of "You Spin Me Round" came up, the girls were firmly into their campy rendition. Sanguine spun around the room as if she were acting out the words. Her long dress floated around her like the waves of an ocean.

Spinning opposite her was the silver skull. The small sculpture made from pieces of eight looked to be drunkenly enjoying the spectacle. Though Kendell knew that was the intention, the song still bugged her. *I'm going to have this friggin' earworm for a month.*

Myles took the guitar from her and set it against the wall. "How did we do?"

Baron Samedi aimed the silver skull at Kendell. "Take it."

She grabbed the trinket. The cane and bones came along with it. Tentatively, she put her other hand on the staff. "It's solid. But what use is it with Marie's hand bones still wrapped around it?"

Baron Samedi took his cane back. "It's a step forward. The magic of Guinee is now available in this hell."

Kendell knew they needed all the help they could get, but the voodoo loa wasn't looking so sharp. "So with it you can return to Guinee?"

He looked up in surprise. "No. You're aware of how the gates are opened. Just because I'm one of the guardians, that doesn't change the fundamental nature of the seven gates."

"I thought this was all about rescuing you."

Myles put his hand on her back. "My job was to get the cane back to Samedi. Your job is to repair this hell so Colin can't just walk out. I'm thinking there's an intersection we might have missed."

She looked at Baron Samedi, hoping for some explanation.

"I'm here to help you," he said. "Agnes Delarosa missed a simple truth about Guinee. Our realm between life and death isn't simply a turnstile to the *deep waters*. Not everyone who dies is ready to have their soul returned to the human continuum. There are seven gates in Guinee for a reason. No one loa is given full power over whether a person can pass or not. Each soul needs to prove itself seven times to move on. Those who fail the tests reside in Guinee until they've learned their life lessons—which some never do. This hell, however, only has one gate back to life, and it's boarded up."

Kendell began to wonder if they'd ever get to leave. "And the old swamp witch makes up this reality, so she's not even a guardian of the gate. That's the secret you didn't want Colin to find out. It's the reason you've stayed in hiding."

He held up the cane. "With this, I can help you build the seven gates from your reality to this hell. Then we can talk about opening the gate to Guinee, but I won't leave this realm until I know you can all safely make it home."

Though she'd visited the seven gates of Guinee to offer libations to the loas for the freeing of Myles, Kendell had no idea how such portals were created. "If we build the gates, we'll give Colin a mission to keep him occupied. That should save me and Sanguine from having our souls battered by him in his attempts to escape. As with the gates to Guinee, just because they exist, that doesn't guarantee that he would be allowed to pass. But how would we even go about creating the gates? And who would man them?"

Baron Samedi lifted the voodoo totem, with her golden pick attached, off the floor and set it on the desk. "This may be the most obvious choice, but I leave scouting out the other six to you."

"But that's a voodoo object. How would that work as a portal between hell and life?"

He ran his finger across the triangle of gold. "This belongs to you. Though it's more than you suspect."

She knew there was more to the gift from the loas than just a way to wail on her guitar. "I've worked with it, but so far, I haven't figured out how to unlock its full powers. Is that what I use to create the gates?"

"As a member of the living, you don't build them. I do. We meant for this object to be your way out of the curse, should you want it. As you guessed, it is a magical box, but instead of having a prize hidden in it, it's a place for you to stash your connection to the Malveaux curse."

From the moment she'd learned about the curse, and her integral part in controlling it, she'd never considered what it would feel like to be rid of the obligation. "I'd be free?"

"Think of it more as your connection to the curse being taken from your soul and kept like a keepsake on a shelf. Only what I'm proposing is that the shelf be kept here in hell. With your voodoo skills, you can check in on it whenever you like, but you'll no longer have the nightmares from hell. And should the time ever come when Colin seeks to be free, and you agree, this will work as your personal gate."

The triangle sat on top of the horrendous wooden head like some kind of miniature French tricorn hat.

"And the voodoo totem would act as a prison should he fail?" Kendell asked.

"It will certainly keep him from bothering you needlessly."

Though she'd grown fond of the expensive token of appreciation, the idea of not being responsible for watching over a devil had its appeal. "Making the connection to the curse was pretty intense. I spent a lot of time barfing in Delphine's voodoo parlor. I'm not sure I'm up for a similar grilling here in hell."

"Delphine de Galpion is only a voodoo priestess. I am a loa of the dead. You can rest assured my powers are superior to hers. This would be the seventh gate from hell to life. Find the other six first. You can decide if it's right for you later."

"What are the requirements for a gate?" Myles asked.

"The gates need to be physical places in this world but also connected to another dimension."

Kendell thought she understood. "So something like the drawing Miss Fleur did of Serephine's eyes."

"I would suggest something more along the lines of the steamer trunk. You'll want your gate to be substantial enough that you're not manifesting onto a soggy piece of rat-chewed paper. There's a reason why the gates to Guinee are burial mausoleums hidden away in cemeteries. Few people are bold enough to vandalize a city of the dead."

Myles paced opposite Baron Samedi behind the desk, a sure sign he was processing his thoughts. "For the sake of argument, say we did use Miss Fleur's trunk. Would that make her the guardian?"

Baron Samedi twirled the cane via Marie's arm bone. "Being a guardian to a gate in hell isn't the kind of job you just want to dump on someone. You'd have to make contact and ask her."

"But she's dead, isn't she?" Polly asked.

"Dimensions—"

Polly raised her hand. "Never mind. I'm pretty sure I don't want to know." For the first time that Kendell could remember, the bandleader meekly took her place against the wall with the rest of the girls.

Kendell began arranging the information in her mind. "Assuming she agrees, then what?"

"Once you have the place and the guardian, draw a veve for each location so I'll know where to look. After you have all seven ready to go, we'll perform our magic. With me helping, the ritual won't be much more involved than what you did here with the cane."

"So long as we get to choose the songs," Scraper mumbled.

12

*K*endell stood on the bank steps, trying to envision all of New Orleans. "Where should we start?"

Scraper ran down the steps, grabbed a rock from under an oak tree, and returned to the group. "Why don't we just make the seven gates out of rocks? We could scatter them all over New Orleans or dump them in Lake Pontchartrain. He'd never find them."

Sanguine took the stone and heaved it back toward the grass border. "Wouldn't work. We'd be in exactly the same situation we're in now. In all religions, redemption must be possible. The gates will have to be places he could figure out. So I guess the question isn't so much where would we start as where would he?"

Myles sat on the step. The dogs quickly circled around him. "If it were me, I'd be looking for where we as his adversaries have been the most comfortable. He'd think we'd be most apt to try to create a gate on our home turf. That dude is all about home-field advantage."

"You're talking about Mary and the Westbank?" Kendell asked.

"In all this craziness, she's been like a mother to you. Even an arrogant prick with delusions of godlike abilities must have had a mother at some point."

Minerva fished out her keys from her pocket. "Let's get going. If she says no, it's back to the drawing board, and I'm already getting frizzy in this hell."

As they crossed the Crescent City Connection, the dark of night gave way to a warm, bright afternoon. Polly sat in front of Kendell with her eyes closed and the sunlight beating down on her cheek. "I'd never get used to living in the dark. I love our night gigs, but I need a little sunshine once in a while to keep the bloom on the rose."

Minerva took the off-ramp with ease compared to the barreling rollercoaster ride of the last time. The she-wolf and her three hellhound pups, who took up every available lap in the vehicle, reverted back to Cheesecake and her puppies. The animals didn't seem to notice the change, but they clearly enjoyed the increased pets and snuggles.

Lynn leaned across the back of the bench seat. "Could Colin even come over here? I'm still confused about this whole no-time experience on that side of the river and why it doesn't hold true on this side."

Kendell looked to Sanguine for an answer.

"If we build the seven gates correctly, my grandmother will let him pass." Sanguine said. "This is his hell, so time only moves when he's learned something important. From reading his notes, he's already figured that out. He'll see it as a positive sign if he can cross the bridge."

Scraper, in the front passenger seat, still didn't seem convinced. "And why do we want him to feel encouraged? Seems like it would be better if he just accepted his fate and stayed holed up in that tower of his. I like Mary. Having him storm over here doesn't seem like a way to keep her safe."

The magnolias were in full bloom and dropped pink and white petals that covered the road. Kendell tried to get past the beauty and stay focused on the devil across the river. "He has to stay focused on trying to get free, even if we never intend on letting that happen. A door that can be opened is more inviting than a brick wall, but if the door looks more like a bank vault, then the thief will go to work with a sledgehammer on the wall."

Sanguine leaned forward. "And when Kendell talks about Colin taking a sledgehammer to his prison walls, she's referring to mine and her souls. This hell my grandmother created requires living spirits to contain the evil. Once she died, the job fell to me and Kendell. We're not just on this joyride to hell to mess with Colin."

Scraper bobbed her head to the side. "Okay, I can see that. But if that fuckface hurts one gray hair on that sweet lady, I'm coming back and beating him to a pulp."

Kendell knew it wasn't an idle threat. The bass player had no problem putting handsy customers in their place at the club. "I'm sure Mary will be glad to hear it, but remember, she's not in this dimension. If he crosses the bridge, I'm sure she'll feel the change in energy. This is her area. She can zap out of this reality as if she were turning off a light switch."

The bus slid to a stop on the gravel driveway. Mary came running down the porch steps before they got the doors open. "Oh, thank God the dogs are with you. When Cheesecake took off running, she nearly gave me a heart attack. Then rounding up the puppies was nearly impossible. It was like they'd had some canine paramilitary training."

Kendell helped Cheesecake out of the bus. "She knows when I'm in trouble. I guess that now goes for Myles as well. The dogs were quite the attack force."

"I'm just glad they, and all of you, are okay. You were gone for a week."

Kendell tried to remember everything they'd accomplished. "It didn't seem that long to us. I wonder how long Colin's been here. Though I guess it doesn't really matter."

"Can I get you some food? You all must be starving."

At the mention of something to eat, all four dogs sat at attention in front of the matronly figure and started wagging their tails with anticipation.

"I feel like I just ate, but something nutritious wouldn't be a bad idea."

Mary pulled off her apron. "Nutritious—listen to you. The food that I make is to revitalize the soul as well as the body."

It didn't take long to explain their plan over the gumbo and sweet tea. Mary listened with all the attention of someone being told how to disable a bomb. "And I would be his first stop?"

"Technically," Myles said, "his first challenge would be crossing the bridge. That should work like a doorbell for your psyche. If he shows up here, you'll have the option of either opening the door or staying in your realm and ignoring him as if he were some door-to-door salesman."

Mary didn't seem convinced. The look she shot Kendell reminded her of the way her mother used to give her the side-eye when she didn't believe Kendell had done her homework. "This is your plan. You would want some say in what goes down, wouldn't you?"

Kendell nudged Myles under the table. He had a much better grasp on how the gates of Guinee worked, and that was the blueprint for what they wanted to create.

He said, "As far as this gate is concerned, you would be the sole guardian. We're not gods—not even loas of the dead. Neither Kendell nor I want to sit in primary judgment of a person's soul."

"So you're breaking up the responsibility, like having multiple judges on a court?"

"Something like that," Myles said. "But we're not asking you to evaluate the man's life, simply one small aspect of it. If you feel he's learned something, you can pass him on. If not, turn him away."

Kendell used the opportunity of Myles and Mary talking to enjoy the gumbo. It lacked some of the surprise the Mary in Kendell's reality mixed into her broth, but then, being nearly homeless required more imagination. This gumbo was much more refined.

"And what should I do if he passes my test?" Mary asked.

Polly dropped her spoon in her empty bowl. "Give him some of this gumbo. This shit's good."

With Mary on board, Kendell headed back out to the bus with the others. Cheesecake and her pups marched along behind her as if they were part of the entourage. The puppies had a way of ramming into the back of Kendell's feet each time she stopped.

"You guys stay here. You all did a wonderful job, but we're not going to be in trouble this time. There's no reason for you all to go demon-puppies on us again."

But Cheesecake wasn't having it. With all the human passengers except Kendell aboard the bus, she launched herself into the packed vehicle and climbed onto Myles's lap. And where their mama went, the puppies followed.

Kendell took a stick from under the oak tree that shaded the house and traced her veve in the dirt. "Once we have all seven locations and guardians, there will be a ceremony. Leave this here until it's over."

Mary gave her another hug with all the warmth and affection of a grandmother. "Be safe. You'll always have sanctuary on our side of the river."

∾

"WHERE TO NEXT?" Minerva yelled from the front seat of the VW. Even without other vehicles, the road noise made it hard to hear her at the back of the van.

Myles held Doughnut Hole tightly and rubbed his ears.

He was going to need all the support he could get. "The Scratchy Dog."

He lurched forward as the brakes screeched the van to a stop. "Why?" The question came from every member of the band, including Kendell.

"Isn't it obvious? If Colin passes Mary's test, that would prove that he's embraced traditional New Orleans culture. His next stop would logically be the club. Live music is ingrained in this city. Who better to represent that than Polly Urethane and the Strippers?" The bus sat motionless on the side of the road.

"He has a point," Sanguine said.

"Bullshit he does." Not surprisingly, Polly was the first to register her objection. He wondered if she'd ever agree to one of his ideas.

"Think about it," he said. "Colin is going to be crossing you women at some point. Making the band the guardians of the second gate means you don't have to wait until the end and make the harder choice. If you accept him, there will be five more chances at rejections. Plus, there are five of you."

"Four," Kendell said. "If I accept Baron Samedi's proposal to be the final gate, I'll have to recuse myself from this judgment."

From the passenger seat, Scraper turned to Myles. "With your girlfriend abstaining, we've got an opening. With four votes, we're likely to be deadlocked—so to speak."

"I'd be honored, but my expertise doesn't extend to music. I'd be useless in knowing whether he was truly appreciating your performance. Anyway, the vote will have to be unanimous for him to move on."

Polly looked at each woman and received nods, though not all were enthusiastic. "We're all in unison, so let's get to the gig."

As the bus crossed the bridge, the adorable two-pound puppy that snuggled against Myles's chest for kisses grew into a fifty-pound monster with short wiry hair. "I don't think I'm ever going to get used to that. You don't think he'll do that when we get back to our reality, do you?"

The dog in Kendell's lap had become a she-wolf three times as big as Doughnut Hole. "I've been a little worried about that. Cheesecake only changes when we're in some other dimension, but these puppies come from hell. Will we even be able to take them home with us?"

He hadn't considered the idea that the pups would somehow be left behind. "Even though Mary offered to take them, you're not going to separate Cheesecake from her little ones. That's just not going to happen. So I guess we'll find out."

Minerva pulled the bus up to what had become their usual parking space right in front of the club.

Lynn did her best to keep Muffin Top the hell beast from slobbering all over her arm. "If we all agree to be gate guardians, what are we doing here?"

Myles found it hard to carry on a conversation with a hellhound on his lap. "It's your home turf. We need to figure out what you'll be dealing with should he arrive."

Kendell handed Cheesecake to Scraper, who was helping clear the beasts from everyone's laps. "Plus, I need to mark the room with the veve so Baron Samedi knows this is the second gate."

Lynn nodded as she got out. "And nothing ever goes exactly according to plan. Got it."

Myles walked into the club that had been the site of so many paranormal events and jumped up onstage. Kendell had the smirk she reserved for moments when she thought he was being stupid. "One little offer of collaboration, and he thinks he's part of the band."

Doughnut Hole jumped up with him and lay at his feet as if to say, *I've got you.*

"I was just trying to envision how he'd approach the band, thank you very much," Myles said. "Mary will get plenty of notice as he crosses the bridge into her dimension, but I suspect he will show up here during a gig—not exactly the ideal situation for being confronted by a devil looking to be freed from hell."

Kendell quickly stopped ribbing him and sat on the edge of the stage, petting Doughnut Hole's head. "You've got a valid point. Is there any way you will be able to detect his presence?"

Myles shared a special connection to Baron Malveaux, who made up a lot of Colin Malveaux's soul, but it wasn't a relationship he wished to remember. "Ever since my possession, I get this feeling across my skin when he's around. It's not goose bumps but more like blind fucking hatred from every cell of my body."

"That should work." She picked up a piece of chalk from the Drink Specials board and started drawing the veve.

He stared at it for a moment. "That's not Baron Samedi's veve."

"I'm basing it on Baron Samedi's symbol, but as the gates are going to be in different places, the map will be different."

He'd thought the drawing was just a means to call the baron forth as they performed the final ceremony. "You're leaving Colin a map? Do you want him to escape?"

"I want him to continue following the breadcrumbs. Plus, if I drew Baron Samedi's veve, our voodoo loa wouldn't know where we've set the gates. It has to be this way to work."

He wasn't so sure. He also had the prickly feeling along his forehead that she wasn't being completely honest. "You're setting a trap."

"I'm covering our bases." She turned to the band. "Though I'll be playing whatever number you decide is appropriate, I'm not part of this gate. It's up to you to decide what you want him to prove."

"That he's not a scumbag." Scraper had a way of cutting to the heart of the matter.

"Fair enough, but what, specifically, does that mean to us?" Minerva asked.

Polly crossed her arms over her stomach. It was a stance that said, *You're not going to like what I have to say.* "He used us. Don't get me wrong—I loved playing Jazz Fest. But his offer was bullshit. He was just trying to outmaneuver us. And he would have, too, if we hadn't been careful."

Kendell hated admitting when others were right. "So he

shows up to the gig but doesn't offer us anything? That seems awfully simple."

"No." Myles paced along the edge of the stage. "He needs to show he's fully enjoying the performance with no ulterior motive—pure admiration for someone else's endeavor with no jealousy or greed."

Polly loosened her stance. "Is that something you can detect?"

"Can't you? I've seen you up onstage. You know when someone's into it, even if they're just sitting in a booth and not out dancing."

"Sometimes that means they're more into it," Polly said. "Someone out on the floor, shaking what they've got, is just crying for attention."

Lynn leaned against the back wall and looked out at the room as though imagining the gig from the audience's perspective. "Assuming he passes our test, which I think highly unlikely, what would we give him as a token of his passing the second gate?"

Everyone stared around the room in silence. Kendell pulled a generic plastic pick from her case. "Though I'm not involved with the judging, do you think it would be okay if I offered the tribute?"

Everyone in the room nodded in approval.

ASKING people to watch over Colin was a bit like serving jury notices, only instead of looking for people who would be impartial, they were seeking out those most concerned about the verdict.

"I want to head back to Minerva's garage," Kendell said. "I've got an idea."

The steamer trunks had been pushed back against the wall but didn't need to be uncovered. Kendell dug down through the gowns for the artist's portfolio filled with pastel drawings of the Malveaux children.

"I don't get it," Scraper said. "If you're going to ask Serephine or Antoine to stand watch, shouldn't we be headed for the Laurette mansion?"

Kendell thumbed through the drawings. She needed one that didn't focus exclusively on just one child. "Miss Fleur was the baron's wife while he was defeating his adversaries and putting their women to work in his brothels. She had to witness her husband's depravity. If Colin accepts New Orleans culture, past and present, then his next stop should be his immediate family."

"But we rescued her when we saved the women Baron Malveaux had imprisoned in Guinee," Polly said. "We saw her cross over to the *deep waters*. How are you going to contact her?"

Kendell pulled out a drawing of a gangly preteen boy and his infant sister. "It's like Baron Samedi said: time doesn't have the same meanings here that we're used to. I'm betting we can contact Miss Fleur while she was in exile in Our Lady of Mercy Convent. Colin will have to face her directly—not as a reincarnation or spectral ghost but as his wife, who'd cloistered herself from everyone she knew."

She held the pastel drawing up to Myles for his

impression. "That should work as her tribute, but our next portal will need to be guarded by both brother and sister."

"I suspect they won't mind sharing the duty."

Myles dropped the lid of the trunk. "Since we can't reach her over my psychometric network, we'll need to haul this thing back to the convent and hope she'll come to us. Kendell can use the drawing as our calling card, but this trunk will act as the gate itself. At least we've got Minerva's bus this time."

KENDELL STRUGGLED out of the tight space of the bus's back seat. "We also need to move the trunk in our reality when we get home. We're not dealing with a different dimension this time, but a connection across time, so what exists at home has to match what's going on here."

Myles was slower at getting out of the bus. "It's not going to be that easy. The nuns were happy to be rid of Miss Fleur's possessions, and I've yet to enter their convent."

The nuns had only been slightly more accepting of Kendell. "If they don't agree to see us, we'll find a way in. We have broken into more secure establishments—in both life and hell."

It took the band handling the trunk while Sanguine pushed from inside to slide it out the back of the van. "This thing weighs a ton. Are you sure she doesn't have some gold bullion hidden in a false bottom?"

Kendell did her best not to lose her hold on the bottom.

"You should have seen me and Myles hauling it over to my apartment."

"I'll stop whining, then. Do you suppose there are any evil nuns guarding the convent in hell?" They dropped the heavy trunk at the front gate.

Myles leaned against thick brick and plaster wall. "That's a really good question. According to Baron Samedi, the convent would be like another embassy in hell. I guess we'll have to knock instead of barging right in."

With no one in sight other than the gang, Kendell felt a little foolish knocking on the old wooden door of the convent. "Funny how fast I get used to a situation. How long do you think we should wait before we try opening the door?"

"I'd give it about a year." The nuns had been much less accepting of Myles.

Kendell giggled at his attempt at humor. "You'll go up against a devil in his own domain, but a couple of sweet little old nuns frighten you?"

The door opened a sliver, just as it had in life. The familiar hard brown eyes looked at her from below the black habit. "You're not welcome here."

"I'm Kendell Summer. This is my boyfriend, Myles. We visited you a few months ago about Miss Fleur."

"I remember you. What do you want?"

Kendell stood back from the opening to show the old woman the trunk. "We need to return this."

"This convent isn't a lending library. You took possession of Miss Fleur's things. That absolves us of any responsibility to her." The door began to close.

"Tell her we're here about her husband, the baron. We've found a way to keep him in hell."

The Reverend Mother's look changed from defiance to curiosity. "Why do you think I can talk to the dead?"

Kendell could tell the woman wasn't from a different dimension. Everything about her looked and felt as real as every member of the group. "Because you're here now. How is that possible?"

The flicker of a smile crossed the woman's face. "How do you think we know when our pupils are misbehaving? We all have our little secrets."

"So you'll help us?"

The old nun looked around at the gang. "It's not our way to join forces with swamp witches and voodoo priestesses, but over the years, Miss Fleur's benefactors have been very generous to our mission. It's just the one trunk?"

With time being such an iffy proposition, Kendell wondered how much of that donated money had been at the bequest of the loas of the dead specifically for this moment. "Yes, sister. And I'll need to talk to her."

The stern woman didn't look happy about the situation. "Very well. Leave the trunk inside the gate and come with me, but only you. Men aren't welcome here."

While they had the trunk off the ground, Kendell discreetly drew the veve on the bottom, where the nuns wouldn't see it. She whispered to Myles, who stood at the side of the gate, "I don't want to push our luck."

Kendell intercepted the band as they left the convent. "You girls should head back to the bank. We need to find out how Baron Samedi is coming along with his end of the ceremony. If I'm doing these veves wrong, I need to know now. Once I'm done with my meeting with Miss Fleur, Myles and I will go to the Laurette mansion to contact Serephine and Antoine. To get there before Colin, though, we're going to need to borrow the bus."

Minerva gave her van a worried look. "Are you sure? We can all stop by the bank together on our way to the Garden District."

Kendell looked adoringly at her demonic dogs, who stood watch outside the van. "We're trying to win over a teenaged boy and his young sister. I don't want to scare the crap out of them. It'll take all of you guys to persuade the pups not to follow the bus."

Minerva nodded slowly and pulled out her keys. "For your own protection, don't take her above thirty-five, and you might want to limit your stops and starts."

13

$\mathcal{C}$olin turned away from his office windows and his search for the VW. Losing sight of the van wasn't what irritated him. "Samedi must have use of that fucking cane. That's got to be it." His sense of what was going on in *his* city was obscured.

The question was whether to go after Baron Samedi, or try to anticipate the meddlesome kids' next move. He could feel his powers being walled off like a game of Tron, and he was playing catch-up.

He headed up to the roof for the best expansive view of the city. From the last dull glow of the van's headlights, he knew the irritating gang was playing out its little plot around the far end of the Quarter. He could reach the bank before they figured out he'd left his tower, but confronting Baron Samedi again felt too much like replaying a losing hand. He turned his back to the only activity in the city. No matter their plan, the amateur gang would eventually head to the Garden District. The fact that they had a vehicle and he had to travel by foot meant he needed to literally stay multiple steps ahead of his adversaries.

He headed down to ground level for the well-traveled path back to the mansion. Serephine wouldn't see him. He'd stopped hoping. For once, he was grateful the worn steps, busted-out windows, and missing wallboards remained exactly as he remembered. He'd kicked the front door in so many times it fell open with only a push of his cane. The driving rain, which forever had just passed, soaked the bottom floor. Every surface squished as he walked through the wreck of a building. "Time to do what I should have done when I first bought you."

His feet slipped on the wet stairs to the open-sided second floor. In the house's arrested state of remodel, moving anywhere above the ground floor felt as though it required a hard hat and steel-toed shoes. The boards were slick with mold moistened by rain. The third floor, however, was close enough to the gabled roof to have remained relatively dry, or at least dry enough, and the rear rooms hadn't been touched. Any financier standing out front of the house and not paying attention would think the crew was farther along than they actually were.

He started pulling small clear jars that contained miniature flames from the inner pockets of his coat. Without their totems, the fire wraiths wouldn't be conscious. Tormenting others would be impossible for his warm, fuzzy pets. But this time, all he needed was their true identity as fire.

He opened each jar and set it next to the most flammable

items he could find: moth-eaten draperies, termite-riddled wood, and peeling wall paper. Without time, the little candles could only illuminate what they were next to. "I'll only need a few minutes to pass."

The air outside felt electric with possibilities. Setting traps for adversaries united both the modern businessman Lincoln Laroque and the manipulating banker Baron Malveaux. Colin felt whole.

He could head back to his offices, but unlike cartoon villains, who never stuck around for the grand finale, he enjoyed watching others suffer. The elegant antebellum mansion across the street had looked down on the Laurette family's estate for over a hundred years. He couldn't imagine a better location for watching it burn.

He walked across the street, feeling he was leaving his past behind. The ornate cast-iron gate soundlessly swung open on its solid hinges as if taunting the derelict across the street. Colin walked five paces before turning back to close the access. "No point in giving away my presence." Months of isolation had made him lazy when it came to closing doors.

A bashed-in door would be an easy reminder that he'd already investigated the premises. He avoided the front door but, for good measure, swung his iron-cane cudgel at a side entry of the mansion. No one would see the damage from the street, and the act of violence helped ease some of the tension that always preceded a confrontation.

Unlike his wreck of a mansion, this home had every bit of molding and railing intact. The pine floors gleamed with fresh finish. Even without furniture, the place oozed class—

like an upscale nude woman who didn't rely on her finery to make an impression.

Colin flipped his cane around and dragged its mangled handle along the floor, knocking out every other baluster along the way. He made his way to the third-floor master suite, scratching, denting, and demolishing as much as he could of the unsullied mansion. The room that faced the street, like the rest of the house, didn't have a stick of furniture. He wished for a chair to sit in while we watched the festivities, but even a devil in his personal hell couldn't have everything.

He didn't have long to wait.

~

Myles wasn't crazy about once again dividing the team and running all over New Orleans with Colin on the loose, but Kendell's concern made a lot of sense. The hellhounds would need everyone to keep them calm.

He doubted the grumpy VW had ever been all that reliable in life, but with Delphine and Professor Yates's modification, the thing positively did not want to start for anyone but Minerva. "At least with there being no such thing as time, the battery probably won't go dead." He gave the key another turn while laying off the gas. The small air-cooled, four-cylinder engine started with a backfire.

Kendell squirmed in the passenger seat. "Please be careful. Minerva will kill me if we damage her precious bus."

Shifting into first gear wasn't a problem. Taking his foot

off the clutch, however, was like releasing a fire-farting dragon, and he and Kendell barely hung on. When he hit the brakes, the big black steering wheel was all that stood between him and the windshield. Without the nice long front end of a normal car, he felt as if he were standing on the frontline of any upcoming obstacle.

"How in the hell does she drive this thing—no air bags, no front end, just a big pane of glass to protect the occupants? This has to be the most unsafe vehicle ever designed."

In response to his disparagement, the bus died at the next corner.

"You really don't know how to talk to a lady, do you?" Kendell stroked the black vinyl dashboard. "It's okay, girl. He didn't mean it. You are a fine old bus with a history anyone would envy. Don't listen to the cruel, mean millennial. You are a hippie chick that will never die."

She nodded at him to try again. The engine spun to life like a little kitten that started purring from having its belly stroked.

"I promise not to say another mean thing." Just to be safe, he treated the van like a cat that couldn't decide if it wanted his attention or was about to scratch the living daylights out of him. He left the bus in first gear for the drive to the Garden District.

The mansion looked like a demented version of the building Myles had worked on with Charlie. "I guess the demon contractor didn't get past the gutting phase."

"Should we knock on the door?" Kendell asked.

If only it were that simple. "I can't see how Antoine or

Serephine could hear us across dimensions. While Colin had me in his little playpen, I was only partially removed from this reality, and I couldn't hear you at all. Did you bring the drawing?"

Kendell held out her hands like a little girl showing she wasn't hiding anything. "I had to leave it in the trunk so Miss Fleur would have it for Colin."

"Right. Damn. I guess we hope Antoine or Serephine find their way to us like Miss Fleur did for you."

As they walked up the path, she took his arm as if she were showing him a piece of property they hoped to buy. It was a silly impression, but one he couldn't shake.

"You've proven pretty good at finding things in this house," she said. "We'll find a way of making contact."

"Let's start with what we know," he said. "Sanguine couldn't have forced Colin into Agnes Delarosa's version of hell without there being a gate. Though we didn't pass through the same location to get here, the gatekeeper had to let us pass. We know that was Antoine, so we know we're welcome." To prove his point, he pushed on the front door, which opened without resistance.

Kendell followed him into the foyer. "We need to contact either Serephine or Antoine. I should have held onto that hair art."

"I considered that. Like Miss Fleur, though, we need to contact her children at a point in their history. By the time Antoine was a Civil War veteran and Miss Fleur made that thing, Serephine had already died."

Kendell began to sound desperate. "There's no way we're finding something from one of them in this mess—

especially not something from them as children. You and Charlie already demolished most of the upstairs."

Myles ran his hand along the wainscot. "As Anthony Laurette, while he was building this place, he used it to hide his connection to his father, the baron, and the associated curse. He didn't dread his sister, though. He loved her. Maybe whatever he had of hers isn't hidden in some moldy, rat-infested attic. He'd have hidden it in a spot more befitting a young girl—someplace very personal."

"You mean like the master bedroom?" she asked.

He looked at her, wondering how she could be so sexy one minute and so naïve the next. "You really think he would have wanted his dead sister's doll under the floorboards of his bedroom? That's just creepy."

"Okay, smarty pants, where would you hide it?"

He turned toward the first door off the hallway. "Do you remember when we were talking with Samantha? We always used this den as the meeting room."

"Sure. It was the main office of Laurette and Associates Architects. It made sense to use it as the meeting room."

He slid the oversized pocket doors fully open. In spite of the run-down condition of the house, the doors moved easily on the hidden rail. "Exactly. Maybe that level of comfort wasn't strictly due to the workspace. Even if the demolition crew had gotten this far, the remodel specified keeping as much of the architectural detail as possible." He ran his hand across the carved moldings that encompassed the magnificent cypress bookcase. "This built-in unit doesn't fit in with the rest of the room. Look around. Everything is made out of either mahogany or oak. This is the only cypress piece in the mansion. Even the carvings are different."

"Please don't tell me we have to destroy it in search of something he hid inside."

He'd spent enough time in the trades to be able to identify work done by a master carpenter. "My bet is this came from the Malveaux family mansion. Mr. Laurette would not have wanted his remembrance of his sister to be sealed off like she was in some cage. He'd want it to be the focal point of the house but only understood by a select few. Something they both might have played in."

"Like a hiding place? It would help if we had some idea of what we're looking for. Do you think the whole wall unit swings open, or is it a miniature compartment?"

He felt the familiar cold chill that preceded an encounter with their enemy. "I don't think it's safe here."

She frowned at him. "Safe in hell? Come on and help me look. You said the bookcase should have some hidden compartment. It's a start at least. Maybe when Serephine and Antoine see we're not leaving, they'll cut us a break."

Trying to entice ghosts out of the walls wasn't a career path Myles had ever envisioned for himself. He climbed the rickety wood ladder that at one time must have made the bookcase truly elegant and started his search in the uppermost corner. Every piece of varnish-peeling cypress still felt substantial enough to warrant a good refinishing. He pulled on each wall section as if trying to remove a book and then checked out the corresponding shelf. Nothing budged.

"This is going to take all day." He looked down from the ladder.

Instead of helping, Kendell was standing in the middle of the room with her hands on her hips. "What's wrong with that cabinet?"

"What are you talking about? I'm not getting off this ladder unless you think you're onto something." The shock at hearing a little girl giggling under his feet made him shake the ladder. "Tell me you heard that."

"It's coming from the cabinet. I think we found what we need."

He eased down the ladder, hoping none of the steps would snap and cause him to fall, landing on the hidden child. Once his feet were on the oak floor, he kept lowering himself until he was looking into the trick-glass front of the cabinet. "It looks like a magician's box." He opened the neighboring door and put his hand inside. He leaned back so Kendell could see it in the angled piece of glass he was kneeling in front of.

"So what, or who, is in *that* cabinet?"

"Good question." He took his hand out and stood up like a parent who'd discovered his child's deception. "Serephine Malveaux, is that you?"

The door popped open, and a child of less than ten years crawled out. "You found me. I knew you would. Antoine said you'd never get it."

As a young man before the Civil War, Anthony Laurette would still be going by his birth name, Antoine Malveaux—the heritage he'd tried so hard to escape once his precious sister took her life.

149

Kendell knelt the way she did when talking to Cheesecake. "Where is your brother? Is he here?"

The girl bit her lip as if she wasn't sure she was supposed to tell. "He's shy. Do you want to see my room?"

Myles could see why the precocious child had been the family's favorite member. "That's a pretty small cabinet. I don't think I would fit."

The joy in her giggle could never be conveyed by Miss Fleur's pastel drawings. "It's just a doorway. My room's on the other side in the old house. I'll go first and pull you through."

Before he could object, she dashed back to the open cabinet. He hurried forward to keep the door to the alternate dimension from closing and turned to Kendell. "Maybe you should go first."

"I suggest a trip to hell, and you're the first on board, but venturing into a little girl's room has you spooked?"

He gave her the scowl he reserved for when he knew she was needling him. "I think you might have more pulling power than a ten-year-old girl. But then, she's not much smaller than you."

Kendell kicked him lightly in the ass for the crack about her diminutive stature. "Just don't let the door shut. I don't want to get trapped in history without you."

With her through the portal, he again had the queasy feeling in his gut telling him something was wrong. The most important thing was to be with her. He reached his arms through the opening. "Pull me through."

A young girl's small hands took his right arm, and Kendell's loving fingers wrapped around his left. With a solid tug, mostly from Kendell, he was on the other side before his nose registered the smell of smoke.

~

SANGUINE COULDN'T GIVE a coon's ass about whether Baron Samedi could use his precious cane. He wasn't her problem —just another interdimensional spirit with delusions of godlike powers.

She walked all four walls of the old bank office, trying to detect her grandmother's magic. The old woman always had something up her sleeve. Re-creating the seventh gate of Guinee wouldn't be any fun if she hadn't left a little surprise for her favorite granddaughter.

The members of the band irritated Sanguine as they fawned over the voodoo loa as though he were a magician at a child's birthday party playing with his phallic-looking stick. This was hell not Metairie. "I don't understand what we're doing here. Someone needs to check on Kendell and Myles. They already talked to Antoine as an adult, so this trip should have been a piece of cake."

Of all the girls, Polly had the most backbone—too bad it didn't connect to a brain. "Kendell knows what she's doing."

That was a laugh. Every plan Kendell dreamed up ended in Sanguine having to swoop in and save the pieces. "I'm telling you, something feels off. I wouldn't be this tense if my grandmother wasn't trying to tell me something."

"Hey, if you're in contact with your granny, can you have her conjure us up a pizza?" Lynn was Sanguine's least favorite band member—too bubbly and flirtatious.

She chose to return to ignoring the whole room. Only Baron Samedi seemed to treat her with the reverence due a swamp witch, but then, he was trapped in her dimension. She supposed she'd be a little more differential to him as well if the situation was reversed.

To everyone else, the walls appeared to be ornately carved reliefs from a bygone era. Sanguine ran her hand over the scene of stately mansions in the Garden District. A smell of carbon mixed with fear manifested in her nose. She leaned down for a better look at the carving, which for her was constantly moving like a wooden hologram. "What was the address of the Laurette mansion?"

No one from the group piped up with an answer, but as she turned to them in frustration, she saw Baron Samedi towering over her. "What do you see?"

"They're in trouble."

He lowered the silver head of the cane to the carving then thrust it hard against the wall. Sparks flew out the bottom tip of the cane.

She knew the place must be on fire, but that wasn't the big surprise. Sprawled on the floor, as if someone had tossed him into the room, was a teenaged boy in 1800s attire. "You have to help. My sister's trapped in the mansion with your friends. The fire started upstairs, but it won't take long to work its way down."

Sanguine knew enough about the hell reality to understand when time moved and when it didn't. Someone, and she didn't need many guesses to figure out who, had masterfully set a trap to hold Kendell, Myles, and Serephine in the same place to allow time to move. "How do we free them?"

Baron Samedi helped the boy off the floor. "Only Antoine can materialize through the relief from office to mansion. I'm still stuck in this office."

Sanguine thought it must be nice not to bear any responsibility, no matter the occasion. "And what the hell are we supposed to do? Carry Mississippi River water with us in our hands? We're not exactly a fire brigade."

"Who cares?" Polly asked. "We need to get there first and do what we can. We're wasting time."

Sanguine could just hear the same words coming from Kendell. "Is it a band thing that you all jump into a fight without first thinking how you're going to win?"

Before Polly had a chance to turn the skirmish into a war, Baron Samedi aimed his cane at the door, which closed tightly. "Sanguine is right. You won't be able to fight the fire. The only answer is stopping time. Sanguine, you're the closest one to this reality. How would we go about halting the fire?"

With a problem in hand and no one to fight with, Sanguine used her brain like a high-speed computer devoid of emotion. "Time moves because the occupant, Serephine, is in intimate contact with people in this realm—Kendell and Myles. From what Antoine said, we have to assume Kendell and Myles can't escape. And the only way to move Serephine away from the mansion is with an object. She's a spirit, like Antoine. Removing Kendell and Myles would be more complicated as they're now in another dimension."

Minerva wasn't the stupidest of the group and for the

most part knew to keep her mouth shut to let others think, but this time, she spoke up. "Can't Baron Samedi stick his cane to the wall like he just did to get Serephine out? It worked for Antoine."

The boy nervously shook his hands. "That won't work. I wasn't with Kendell and Myles. On my own, I could escape. Sere would feel obligated to stay even if she could leave."

Much as Sanguine hated to admit it, Polly's criticism about wasting time was starting to ring true. "You girls get going. Take the dogs. They proved pretty useful last time. My guess is Colin's playing with fire again. Baron Samedi, Antoine, and I will find a way to remove Serephine from the mansion, which should make the fire stand still."

Lynn looked like someone who'd just gotten the punch line to a joke someone had told hours earlier. "Is that why Madam de Galpion's shop and the Scratchy Dog didn't burn? But how come the wraiths still got to torment us?"

Polly grabbed the confused girl's arm. "All very good questions—for another time."

Once the distracting women had left, Sanguine turned to Baron Samedi. "To call Serephine forth, we'll need one of her possessions. As we know, those are currently in the convent. And I'm guessing you can't bring your magic wand onto church grounds."

"She needs to manifest here. This was her father's office and, more importantly, a crossroads of dimensions. She and Antoine are safe here or at the mansion, but nowhere else."

Dammit. "Right. I'll be back as fast as I can. Be ready."

As Sanguine ran through the Quarter, she wondered if a swamp witch would be any more welcome at the convent than a voodoo loa of the dead. The physical exertion helped drive the self-doubt from her mind. She'd bust the door down if she had to.

When the abbey walls came into view at the end of the street, Sanguine had lost all patience. She didn't even slow down as she lifted her feet and slammed her side against the solid door. "Open up right now!"

She backed up and launched her body at the door again. "I don't have time for your shenanigans. There's a fire, and I need something you have."

As she ran at the door for the third time, it opened a crack. The gap grew considerably larger when her hundred-and-fifteen-pound muscular body hit the center of the door.

The old Mother Superior lay flat on her back inside the gate. "Excuse me. You're not welcome in here."

Sanguine really couldn't have cared less what the old woman thought was appropriate decorum in her grandmother's realm. "Where's the trunk we just dropped off? I need something out of it, and I don't have time to discuss the matter."

The woman pointed toward the Spanish-style sanctuary. "My novices dragged it into the rectory. But you won't be able to enter."

"And why the hell not?"

The woman struggled to her feet, regaining her dignity in the process. "Because, witch, this is holy ground. Outside, you might have the protection of your demon grandmother, but inside one of our buildings, you're at our command. Tell me what you're looking for, and I'll get it for you. But don't for a moment think this is part of your domain."

For Sanguine, taming her enthusiasm was like trying to get her hair to behave—possible, but not without casualties. "There's a folder of drawings. I just need one of a young girl. That's it."

The old woman motioned her to follow. "You could have just asked."

~

COLIN RESISTED DANCING around the room like a foolish schoolboy who'd just set fire to his sister's Barbie Dream House. But the fact was, he couldn't have envisioned a better outcome.

Not that he could see the flames across the street. In that reality, time was moving forward. His would stand still until some benevolent being allowed it to progress. That didn't mean, however, that he didn't have his little spy.

The flame in the blue-glass jar that he left in the middle of the room leapt out of the narrow opening and shot halfway to the ceiling, mirroring what its brothers were experiencing in the house across the street. Colin looked back out the window and tried to estimate how much of the mansion would be engulfed. All the while, he kept an eye on the front door to see if that spunky guitarist and her dolt of a boyfriend had figured out their predicament.

Though he felt a momentary pang of regret at having missed his chance to bed the girl, she'd become too much of a pest for him to keep up his little games with her. The boyfriend, however, would be no great loss to anyone.

He heard the running footsteps and cries of "Kendell!" and "Myles!" before seeing the four women racing down the center of the street.

"Foolish girls. You're in my dimension. What did you think you were going to see—a raging inferno?"

He crossed his arms in smug satisfaction as he watched the women's looks of confusion. They'd be staring at the same run-down house—no flames, no falling timber, and most of all, no Kendell and Myles.

Their voices carried clearly up to him in the otherwise silent neighborhood.

"What do we do?" the short brunette asked in a childish panic.

The tall blond singer he'd seen onstage was a little too blatant with her sexuality for his tastes, but she had a lovely voice even when not singing. "Only the top two floors look burned. If I've understood that crazy witch and loa, what we're seeing will remain this way for us. So we go inside and see if we can determine the cause of the fire. Maybe we can find some drapes or something to smoother it out."

"Wouldn't work, Polly. The fire would just stay there like it was painted on the walls," said the tall, thin, butch-looking woman with the shaved head. He'd never cared much for her.

The four women stood there like silly children trying to summon up enough bravery to enter a haunted house during Halloween. He looked at the mansion again, trying to see the damage to the top two floors. To him, the sections looked as they always had. "Interesting. So you can see farther ahead in time than I can. How can I make that work to my advantage?"

The blonde took off at a run. "The mansion is in this arrested state of demolition. If we knock out the downstairs doors and walls, maybe Kendell and Myles can escape in their dimension. Even if they aren't with us, at least they won't get stuck in a burning building." The others chased after her.

He gripped the top of his iron cane. Even if he could catch up to them, it'd be one man against four much more agile women. "It won't matter. Even if that pair escape, they won't be darkening my hell again. I can live with them being in some other realm."

Just the same, he turned to the door to pursue the women. Standing in the shadowed opening were three beasts with glowing red eyes and baring razor-sharp teeth.

"Away with you, creatures. This is my realm, so you are under my command."

But the animals continued to creep into the room. With military control, two took up flanking positions along the sides while the all-black leader continued his direct, slow attack.

"I'm not afraid of you. Did Baron Samedi conjure you up like that she-wolf at the bank?"

Unlike that creature, these three thinner and meaner-looking demons didn't have someone calling them off. The two bitches triangulated their approach. Arrogance only worked to a point. If he couldn't bluff, he'd have to fight.

From years of corporate experience, he knew he had to go after the leader.

Colin held his iron cane like a baseball bat with the handle adding weight and menace to the end. "All right, you want to dance? Show me what you've got."

But the animal didn't take the bait. He glowered toward the floor, taking aim at Colin's ill-healed leg.

"Smart boy. Figure out an enemy's weakness and let him know you know. But you've miscalculated."

From his left, the tan-and-black-camouflage bitch lunged at his hip.

He had to swing the metal bar close to his side to catch her in the jowl, but her momentum managed to drive her teeth into his arm. Blood began gushing from the four punctures.

The animal whined at being struck but showed no signs of giving up her post. The black leader didn't chastise her. He didn't even look in her direction. Like a military general, he'd watched the encounter to determine his opponent's tactics.

Colin backed closer to the window. Escape wasn't his best course of action. The girls might be in the house, but the loud commotion would bring them outside. He didn't care about being discovered, but being so fully outnumbered could end badly for him. His heel struck the window molding. He was the proverbial cornered animal, and that made him dangerous. Like a baseball player warming up on deck, he swung the metal bar in a full arch.

The three animals were just out of range. His show of

strength hadn't impressed any of them, not even the one with blood oozing from the open wound on her jaw.

The muscles of the black leader's shoulders and haunches rippled. Colin knew what the animal was thinking. He'd been there many times in the boardroom and remembered that luscious first scent of fear. The moment had come for the attack, and there was no way Colin could take on all three animals.

While still holding the metal club menacingly at the animals, he knocked the foot of the cane against the base of the large window. The mostly ornamental latch gave way with only one firm shove. "Okay, boy. I'm headed out this window. Hopefully, that's all you want."

He turned and dove through the opening with more agility than he'd displayed since college. From two stories up and landing on grass that was more marsh than lawn, Colin only lightly bruised his arm, though his rib again burned. He headed down the street, not bothering to wait and see if the hell creatures were interested in following.

"This is bad, really, really bad." The poor child had her arms around her knees and was rocking forward and back in the corner of her room.

Kendell couldn't stand to see her so afraid. "We're in your reality now. You won't be hurt here."

"You don't understand. Antoine will be stuck in father's hell." Her large azure-blue eyes glistened. "And you two won't have a way back."

Kendell turned to Myles. "Are you sure you smelled smoke? I mean, I might be a little musty after all this non-time stuck in Colin's hell."

Serephine wasn't having any distraction. "No, it's on fire. I can feel it. The magic mirror must have broken from the heat. Antoine would be here if our cabinet wasn't broken. This is our home. We shouldn't have been playing with that stupid magic door. I knew that woman was going to bring us trouble."

Kendell didn't want to give Serephine more to worry about, but Agnes Delarosa had a lot of damn nerve using a young, innocent child as part of her gate from life to hell. She curled up behind the girl and tried to hold her tightly, but her arms went right through the small body.

"I told you this is bad. You're here in spirit, but your bodies are still in that magic box in the burning house. Just like how I was there in spirit but solid here."

Kendell started to really get worried, but she couldn't let Serephine see that fear. "We have friends in that world. Antoine will have help. From what I know of him, he seems to be a very smart man."

"He's brilliant, but he's not yet a man. And father is scary no matter what world he's in. This is bad."

She could tell the girl was about to break down. Unable to hold her, Kendell did the next best thing she could think of. It hadn't been the first song she'd ever learned, but "Bridge Over Troubled Water" was the song her mother sang when Kendell was scared. Singing it quietly to Serephine helped ease both their fears.

Myles knelt against the wall as she finished the song.

"Sing another one. What was that piece you used to play for Cheesecake when she wasn't feeling well?"

She could tell he wasn't asking for entertainment purposes. "What did you hear?"

"It'll sound stupid, but I thought I heard Cheesecake trying to sing along. You once told me Polly could pick out a tune in just a couple of notes. Think she could figure it out if it was in doggy language?"

Kendell began to get excited. "If she does, she can have one of the girl puppies." She turned back to Serephine, who didn't seem to understand what was going on. "I'm going to sing a song that was very special to my dog. We think she's on the other side of your magic door. If my friends are with her, we might be able to open a link."

"I won't be able to go with you." Serephine got up so fast Kendell checked to make sure the floor wasn't on fire. "My brother's calling me. But I can't leave you two in danger. It's my fault you're here."

Myles stayed on his knees so he could talk eye to eye with the girl. "This isn't your fault. You're a very brave little girl. Check first to make sure he's safe. Can you tell?"

Serephine cocked her head to the side. "He's in Father's office. He's not alone, but it's not Father he's with."

Myles put his hands next to the girl's feet. "It's okay. That's our friend. He can look a little scary, but he's here to help. We'll meet up with you as soon as we're free. Thank you for showing us your room."

While he was assuring the girl, Kendell had taken his spot close to the wall and begun singing "You've Got a Friend."

Serephine turned to her and pointed toward some loose beadboard. "It's opening."

First to stick her nose through the opening was Cheesecake the she-wolf. Serephine screamed loudly, and Kendell heard a voice from the other side, demanding to know if everyone was all right.

"It's okay. That's just my dog. I know she looks scary, but she's not really."

As if to prove Kendell's point, the fearsome beast who could only get part of her head into the room looked up at Serephine and gave a playful "woof" that she reserved for her puppies.

"You see. We're going to be okay. You can go. We'll see you as soon as we can."

~

MYLES HATED the smell of smoke that permeated every stitch of his clothing and would probably stay there until he got back to his own reality, where time and baths existed. As he stood outside, he held Kendell tightly. She smelled equally sooty. "That was closer than I'd have liked."

Everything above the ground floor of the house was in full blaze, and the room they'd been yanked out of had boards falling from the ceiling. "Yikes. You girls dove into *that?*" Even Cheesecake snuggled against Kendell's side at the sight.

Polly sniffed at her clothes. "It wasn't that bad when we went in."

Myles wondered if he'd ever adjust to how time

jumped the rails in this reality. "Let's get out of here. I want to see what Baron Samedi, Sanguine, and Antoine came up with to save Serephine." He looked again at the burning-building tableau. "I guess we'll need to find another gate."

He happily returned the car keys to Minerva before climbing in the back of the van. It felt like a week had passed since he'd driven the thing.

Cheesecake took her usual spot across his and Kendell's laps. He gave her a big hug. "You did amazing, girl. Hey, where are your pups?"

Polly turned to look at him from the front seat. "As we came up the street, they snuck into a yard across from the Laurette mansion. They looked like they were on a mission, so we didn't disturb them. Those dogs have their own agenda, and at this point, I'm inclined to go with whatever they have in mind."

He had to agree with her assessment, but that didn't make him less nervous about what the puppies were up to. "They are going to be a handful when we get home."

The bank looked quiet enough as the bus rolled to a stop out front. Though the peaceful scene meant Myles and the group weren't diving into another conflict, it also meant that action was probably going on elsewhere.

Kendell pulled Myles from the back seat. "I want to make sure Serephine made it safely. I can't stand the idea of her being stuck in that burning building."

They ran through the dark bank to the upstairs office. Kendell nearly broke the latch on the door as she burst into the room. Baron Samedi and Sanguine were working on some mystical incantation at the desk while the two youths sat quietly on the large leather couch.

"You two are okay?"

Serephine got up to speak for her and her brother. "We were waiting on you. Baron Samedi and Antoine were able to pull me from the picture of the bank in my room through the carving of our house on the wall." She pointed to the engraving on the wainscoting.

Though Myles was relieved that everyone had escaped, the demolition of the Laurette mansion did interfere with their plans. "So now we have the guardians but no gate."

"I'm not sure I'd call a teenager and his younger sister sufficient guardians of a devil." Polly was never very diplomatic.

Antoine stood up and took his sister's hand. "I know we appear as children, but I have all the memories I acquired in life, including how I prevented my father's curse from ruining my family. We don't need to physically fight him, only remain true to what we remember. He can't bully us."

Polly didn't seem convinced. "Perhaps you have enough hatred to carry you through thousands of years as protector of the gate, but what about your sister?"

Serephine looked up at her brother before answering. "We're two sides of the same coin. Father will have to prove to Antoine that he's not a threat." She looked back to the bandleader with her light-blue eyes. "And he'll never be able to lie with me present."

Unlike Polly, Myles hadn't worried too much about how the baron's children would judge their father, but he had other concerns. "That still leaves us without a gate."

Baron Samedi looked wan behind the desk. "This office was even more a part of the baron's life than the mansion. His children, be they bodies or spirits, are welcome in this place. With the connection they have with the pictures in their rooms, they can manifest in this office to do their work. And as this is also the seventh gate of Guinee, I can provide them cover. Should Colin make it to the fourth gate of hell, I'll be here to guide his children."

Myles suspected overlapping different belief systems might have some negative side effects. "Doesn't that create a conflict of interest?"

"To create the seven gates, you're going to need a little Guinee magic. Establishing where they are and who is guarding them is just the beginning. The ceremony to unite the gates only works if I give them my blessing. And I can only do that if I can access my powers. By having the seventh gate of Guinee line up with your fourth gate to hell, I can bridge the two realities."

From the way the loa looked, Myles wasn't sure he could bridge a storm gutter, let alone two realms. "You have your cane, but Marie Laveau still has her hand wrapped around it."

Baron Samedi turned the staff as if checking to see that the bones were still attached. "She isn't blameless when it comes to Baron Malveaux and the theft of my cane. She'll go along if she knows what's good for her."

Myles was pretty sure he didn't want to know what the threat would entail when it was directed toward someone who'd already passed to the *deep waters*. "So how will this work?"

"When every gate and guardian is in place, I'll shoot a beam of green light toward the heavens. The guardians will see it." He pointed the staff at Kendell. "That will be your sign to begin singing. The connection will allow you to see everyone in all seven gates. When they acknowledge your song, you'll know they are a part of the whole."

Kendell paced the way Myles often did when he was thinking. "I'm still uncomfortable with the connection between Guinee and our gate to hell. It sounds like a railway station servicing unmarked trains traveling in differing directions."

"It's not ideal, but so long as Wicca and voodoo don't conflict with each other, the intersection won't be an issue. Someone progressing through the previous six gates of Guinee won't be traveling the same direction as someone who's passed the three gates of hell."

Kendell crossed her arms. "And if they do end up in conflict?"

"Then it will take a voodoo priestess and a Wiccan witch to mediate a compromise."

Sanguine had a worried look on her face. "I suppose it's the best we can do at the moment."

As Kendell drew her veve on the underside of a desk drawer, Baron Samedi passed the pastel drawing to the children. "This is your validation. Should the time come when you do believe what your father tells you, giving him this will be your way of formalizing your acceptance."

Serephine looked at her mother's drawing. "What if he just steals it?"

The question was so simple Myles wondered why no

one else had thought of it. Baron Samedi let out a heartfelt laugh that belied his deteriorating condition. "It wouldn't matter. The symbol is only valid if you've first given your consent. If he took it, he wouldn't be able to get through the remaining gates."

14

Myles wasn't crazy about the fourth gate matching up to Baron Samedi's seventh gate to Guinee, but establishing the portal put the gang one step closer to getting out of hell. "Where to next?"

Baron Samedi leaned on the cane as he stood from the chair. He looked to have lost half of his weight. "If I could offer a suggestion? Behind the Scratchy Dog is an outdoor bar. During Prohibition, it was used as a speakeasy. People like confiding in their bartenders."

Everyone turned to Myles. "Me? I'm not sure that's such a good idea. I've already crossed paths with Malveaux in the spirit world."

"That's what makes you the perfect gate guardian," Baron Samedi said. "For Colin to prove to you that he's rehabilitated would be no simple matter."

The voodoo loa had a point. Myles couldn't envision

ever giving his permission for Colin to leave hell. "What about the rest of the process?"

Baron Samedi switched from leaning on his cane to leaning against the desk. "Doughnut Hole has a connection to the club. He'll know when something's not right. As for your token, I'd suggest a shot of something. For my sake, just don't make it rum."

Even though the pup had been instrumental in saving the band, Myles wasn't sure that was the connection Baron Samedi was referencing. "If Colin gets past me, I'll make him a Sazerac. Okay, I'll do it. I suppose we're kind of running out of gates and guardians. But before we go racing back to the club, I want to find the dogs. If Doughnut Hole is going to be a part of this process, he's got a right to be present. Any guesses on where they might be?"

Baron Samedi handed his cane to Kendell. "As Cheesecake's owner, you're the closest human to the puppies. Take this around the room. The reliefs carved into the walls will indicate their location. With all of us here, I have to believe the dogs are keeping an eye on Colin."

Kendell took the cane and slowly pointed the silver skull at every engraved, three-dimensional mural. The Garden District, Algiers, and the French Quarter all displayed only the wooden carvings with no indication of activity.

"Where could they be?" She looked to Myles. The action caused her to swing the cane toward a far corner of the room.

"Look there, past the Bywater. He's leading the dogs across the Industrial Canal."

Kendell hurried to that side of the room and put the

cane against the relief of the bridge. "Why would he be headed for the Lower Ninth? I can't imagine he ever had any dealings over there."

Myles watched the hologram that projected from the end of the cane. Colin was struggling across the open grating of the drawbridge section while the dogs worked the sides and middle of the approach. "That neighborhood wasn't to be entered casually even in life. In hell, it might make for an impressive trap."

Polly got so close to the projection that a wall of the shipping lock displayed across her face. "He keeps looking back to make sure the puppies are following. We have to go save them." Though Myles knew the hellhounds' origin, having Polly remind everyone that they were actually cute little balls of fur only created more panic.

Sanguine took the end of the cane and moved it farther into the area that had been decimated too many times by hurricanes. "I don't see a lot of dry land. If I didn't know better, I'd say the houses had been dropped in one of the area's swamps."

"And where there are swamps," Lynn said, "there are alligators."

Sanguine said, "Normally, my biggest concern would be the human population, but without people—and Colin having some knowledge of working in this realm—trained gators are a possibility. I'd be more concerned with snakes, nutrias, and packs of wild dogs." As both a resident of the bayou and the expert on her grandmother's creation, she had more knowledge of this than anyone.

Myles didn't see any overt threat, but any good trap

would be well camouflaged. "He wouldn't be leading them over there just to get even with his attackers. He's too clever to let his desire for revenge distract him. We're closing the noose around him, and he knows it."

Kendell set the cane down. "You think he wants us to follow him?"

"I think he wants us to stop building the gates. We've already seen what he's capable of accomplishing. Once again, he's showing us he can hold our dearest friends ransom."

Polly kept fidgeting. "What does it matter? I'm not going to sit around and let him hurt the puppies. Who's with me?"

Lynn immediately jumped to Polly's side. Myles knew Minerva and Scraper would follow their bandleader if he didn't do something fast. "The Scratchy Dog is on the way. We'll stop off so Kendell can make her mark, and then we'll head across the canal. I don't want our group splitting up this time. We're stronger together. Colin isn't going to harm the dogs so long as he can use them as bargaining chips."

Baron Samedi took back his cane. "I and the Malveaux children can keep tabs on you from here, but I fear there isn't much we can do should you get into trouble."

"As always," Myles mumbled.

DESPITE ALL OF THE TRAVELING, getting into and out of the old VW bus never got any easier for Myles. Even though he wasn't part of the band, the Scratchy Dog was beginning to feel like a second home to him.

Scraper led the way past the bathroom to the courtyard behind the club. "When we first started playing gigs here, I'd sneak out back for a smoke. The alleyway's been cleaned up for customers, but this back hideaway is still used for storing junk."

As was her nature, Polly took charge. "Everyone spread out and start digging through this crap toward the walls. I doubt the speakeasy would be hidden inside a brick wall, so concentrate on the areas that look like they might be hiding boarded-up doors."

Myles took the section piled high with pallets. "Might have been nice if the swamp witch had made this place empty like the rest of the city."

Sanguine gave him a hand, tossing the rotted wooden structures into the middle of the open space. For a skinny girl, she had considerable strength. "Any place that we're connected to is kept as precise as possible. That's how she establishes the *embassies*, as Baron Samedi called them."

"So this place connects to our reality?" he asked.

"More or less. I mean, just because we're tossing these pallets here in hell, that doesn't mean they're magically flying through the air in life. But don't be surprised if you get home and find the manager had an unexplained hankering to clear out this back space."

He looked at the locked-down storm shutters that had been hidden under the pallets. "Dead end."

Kendell was busy measuring the space by walking heel to toe across the courtyard. "I'm not so sure. If you compare where the back door is relative to this wall, the men's room inside the club would have to be about five feet deep."

"Have you seen the urinal?" Myles asked. "There's not a lot of room to do one's business."

"Humor me and open the shutters," Kendell said.

With no one in the neighboring building, he wasn't concerned about peeking into someone else's establishment. It took a good couple of hits from a rock to break the old rusty locks. He lifted the brown shutters, expecting to see painted-shut windows. Instead, sandwiched between the opening and the wall was a narrow serving counter with barely enough space for a person behind it. He shimmied over the counter. A little searching revealed a couple of well-hidden bottles of alcohol behind the built-in metal trashcan. For a gate between hell and life, he could have done far worse.

"This must be the place," he said. "There's not much room, but you could make your veve under the counter."

Polly was already leading the way back to the bus. "Now can we save the puppies?"

THOUGH SHE PRIDED herself on knowing every aspect of New Orleans, the Lower Ninth Ward was an area of the city Kendell usually avoided like any normal middle-class white girl. Her bohemian-goth bravado ended at the drawbridge.

Once they'd crossed into the desolation of the Lower Ninth, Myles put his hand on Minerva's shoulder. "Let us out here. Kendell, Sanguine, Cheesecake, and I will sneak down toward the river. You drive the rest of the band up along the levee and start your grid search, working your way toward us. If you see the pups in trouble, lay into your horn."

"And if you guys end up snared in his trap?"

Myles shook his head with more confidence than Kendell felt. "We won't. I've been here before, which gives me an advantage over Colin. If he is using the swamp animals as his attack force, he'll be in for a surprise. As both a swamp witch and the granddaughter of this hell's designer, I'm betting Sanguine can charm these animals without trying. Plus, Cheesecake knows her pups. I'm hoping he'll pursue you, giving us time to find the dogs."

Once out of the bus, Myles motioned them toward a vacant lot lined with a vine-covered fence and trees draped with Spanish moss. "When I came over here searching for Professor Yates, I made the mistake of starting near the river. With the docks and the nicer homes, that area felt more inviting. As someone who has lived his life in the city, Colin would also gravitate toward these buildings instead of wandering out toward the less habitable areas."

Even with all the flooding, the warehouses along the river were high and dry. "Why was that a mistake?" Kendell asked.

"I wasn't looking at it from the perspective of a kidnapper." He pointed along the Mississippi River then perpendicular to that, along the Industrial Canal. "To start with, escape from those buildings is limited unless he has a boat, which seem awfully scarce in this hell. Even without anyone around, the cleared lots make for less secluded hiding. Finally, if the pups are being held on one of the docks, their barks will carry from the elevated, cavernous warehouse."

Kendell still didn't like having to trudge through the marshy empty lots. "Have you considered that the puppies might have cornered Colin? They are pretty clever."

"If that's the case, this will be an easy rescue. Colin's not the type to be tricked twice by the same adversary, though. Doughnut Hole and his sisters have gotten the drop on Colin a couple of times now. Even if Colin is not out for retaliation, he'd be focusing all of his cunning on showing them who's in charge in hell. Plus, we know he's fond of setting traps."

Though Kendell didn't enjoy having her hypotheses so easily disproved, she liked having a boyfriend who, when the need arose, could be an intellectual equal. "Do you really think he'll head out after the van?"

"The first thing we need to know is if the pups are in one of the warehouses." He turned to Cheesecake. "That's where you come in, girl. I don't pretend to understand how you and your brood are figuring things out, but you all seem to know exactly where to be and when. Stick with us, but if you sense your puppies are nearby, let us know."

Kendell appreciated that Myles acknowledged Cheesecake's important roles in their adventures.

He turned to Sanguine. "He'll have some kind of protection, and that means either animals or snares. You're our expert on both."

The young swamp witch nodded. She stood a little straighter now that she was back in her element among the wild plants and hidden animals. "He's no expert on living off the land. I'll spot any of his crude attempts at building a trap."

"Good. If all goes well, he'll find himself trapped between four angry dogs, six pissed-off women, and me."

Kendell knew that Myles was at least as pissed off as the rest of them. The baron's possession of Myles's body was a debt that still called out for reckoning. "And if you're wrong?"

"You mean if he's smarter than I was and isn't down by the docks where we can easily find him? Then hopefully Minerva and that noisy bus will either flush him out or cause the puppies to start barking so we can sneak up on him from behind."

Having Cheesecake lead the way helped ease Kendell's fears of running into a creature from hell. Even with both Myles and Sanguine's explanation that the young swamp witch would be able to command any animal that they ran across, Kendell couldn't stop imagining hell beasts with the old swamp witch's dead eyes, attacking anything they ran across. With Sanguine following Cheesecake, at least she'd be in a position to combat anything they ran across.

The she-wolf kept to the shadows as they left the tangled jungle of a neighborhood for the equally terrifying warehouse of horrors. Kendell tried to keep her thoughts in line, but hell had a way of coloring her thinking with shades of fright.

Sanguine put out her hand in warning. Everyone, including Cheesecake, hugged the side of the warehouse as the swamp witch peeked around the corner. She turned back and whispered, "Gators. Big ones."

Kendell wasn't sure if she should feel terror at the prospect of facing hell gators or relief that they may have found the puppies and Myles had been right. Her heart decided to triple its rhythm just to cover all bases.

"Stay here," Sanguine whispered. "Time I found out what I can do with my grandmother's pets."

Kendell held tight to Cheesecake's mane to keep the wolf from doing something foolish. Myles knelt to the dog-wolf's head. "Any indication of your pups?"

Cheesecake gave him a kiss, then two kisses, and finally three.

He looked at Kendell. "I'm going to interpret that as a yes."

She nodded. "That still doesn't tell us where Colin is, though."

"One threat at a time." He joined her at the corner of the warehouse to spy on Sanguine and the two ten-foot alligators that were lounging on the wooden pier.

The swamp witch moved in slowly. The animals got off their bellies. Their beady red glowing eyes swiveled to her like laser beams. For a moment Kendell was certain they were going to lunge at her, but as she moved in closer, they turned toward the water.

"Stop." Sanguine's command was quiet enough not to be heard within the warehouse but strict enough to halt the gators where they stood. "You obey me now. I will call you Right, and you Left. Take your positions."

To Kendell's amazement, the two monsters lumbered next to Sanguine. The success seemed to have gone to the swamp witch's head. She yelled, "Let's go get those puppies."

Colin Malveaux stepped out of the shadows of the open truck bay and faced Sanguine. "You think maybe I didn't expect you? Those two are the laziest animals I've encountered in my hell. The snakes, however, are far livelier."

"Makes sense that he relates to snakes since he is one." Myles's attempt at humor almost made Kendell laugh, which would have given away their location.

"Now, where are your compatriots?" Colin asked. "I don't for a minute believe you came here all on your own."

Sanguine patted the two gators' scaly heads. "I think you underestimate my friends." As she moved toward him, her guardian gators kept pace.

"She's not talking about the swamp creatures," Kendell whispered. "She meant us."

Colin casually swung his iron cane. "I wouldn't come any closer. Even if you can control the animals here, I've got quite a few snakes slithering guard around those hellhounds. Took me longer than it should have to realize they're connected to that she-wolf. If I were to take a guess, I'd say they must be that old, overweight lapdog and the bitch's bastard offspring. Hell has a way of changing people and dogs."

It took all of Kendell's strength to keep Cheesecake from attacking. "Not yet, girl. He's just trying to get under your coat."

Sanguine sauntered closer. "Not a bad guess, and I won't insult your intelligence by pretending the dogs don't matter to us all. We're just looking to get them back."

179

He leaned on his cane with both hands. "So we're up to the negotiation stage."

"Good," Myles said. "She's got him thinking he has the upper hand by playing into his business skills."

Kendell clamped her hand to her mouth to prevent a scream when a black snake slithered across her foot.

Myles patted Cheesecake's haunches. "I think Sanguine may have sent us a guide to where the puppies are being kept. Let's see what door the little guy slinks under."

All she could envision was some horror story involving a building filled with snakes. "How do you know this one's from Sanguine and not Colin? Seems like the kind of trickery he'd dream up."

Myles nodded at the black silhouette of the VW bus as it crept up the street. "Have Minerva back the van to the warehouse door. I'll slip in with Cheesecake and our little slithery friend. If that snake is two-timing us, you'll be able to rescue me. If not, I'll bring the puppies out."

"I don't want you to leave me."

He leaned in to give her a heartfelt kiss. "I'll only be a minute."

KENDELL WATCHED Cheesecake follow Myles as he crept up a loading ramp after the undulating black serpent. Having them both face potential danger made her freeze in place. *I could still chase after them.*

"There you are." Polly had snuck up behind Kendell.

Grateful not to be alone, she hugged the bandleader. "We

think the puppies are in that warehouse. Sanguine has Colin distracted for the moment, but we don't have long. What's with the silent bus? That thing can usually be heard from a block away."

"Minerva found a stealth mode on that old jalopy. She pushed the light button in too hard, and the thing went silent. Apparently, Delphine made some changes she didn't tell us about. We can sneak it right up to the loading bay."

Worried as Kendell was about Myles and Cheesecake, she was glad to know that they had the support of the band. "Get in position, and listen for Cheesecake. If there's a problem, send someone to get me. I need to check on Sanguine."

Kendell stayed hidden next to the corrugated metal wall until she saw the black shadow of the VW merge with that of the neighboring warehouse. *One conscious human snake is worse than a hundred mindless ones. They'll be okay so long as Colin doesn't know what we're up to.* The rationalization gave her enough strength to turn her attention to helping Sanguine.

As she peeked back down the alley toward the river, though, both Colin and Sanguine had disappeared. *Fucking great. Now I have to go after her.* She began to understand why Myles made lists of things to do. He wasn't so much trying to make sure he didn't miss something as steeling himself for the tasks ahead.

She kept low and ran across the short open space between the two buildings. Even the two monstrous alligators had vanished, though Kendell wasn't worried about them. Great lumbering beasts with jaws that could crush her motor scooter weren't nearly as frightening as coiled black ropes in the shadows pretending to be snakes, ready to strike.

Time was not on her side, and her fears—rational and otherwise—would just have to bugger off. Focusing as much energy as she could on picking up any random sound, she worked her way under the raised loading dock.

"I'm going to ask you again: where are your friends? And don't get smart with me this time." Colin's tone of command from inside the warehouse confirmed that Sanguine had gotten herself into a mess.

"You and your little pet worms can just fuck off."

Apparently, she either hadn't been bitten or didn't care. Kendell thought the latter more likely. Having lived out in the bayou, Sanguine would have dealt with more than the occasional water moccasin.

"You won't give in to fear. I can respect that. Your grandmother taught you well. I wonder how you'd feel about seeing one of those hell puppies tortured."

"Death is a part of life."

Kendell knew Sanguine well enough to detect the slight waver in her voice, indicating a bluff.

With Colin focused on interrogating Sanguine, Kendell climbed onto the concrete bay for a better look. The two gators lay against the walls on either side of the roll-up metal door like marble sentries. Each shook its head in warning at her approach.

Fuck you, Sanguine. I'm not leaving you alone in there. Kendell crept close to the left side of the opening, away from the voices, and rounded the wall. The full moon shone in the building's skylight, illuminating her friend, who was secured, spread-eagled, to two metal beams. The ropes around her wrists and ankles never stopped moving. *Fuck you and your snakes.* Kendell imagined that if Colin ever escaped his hell, he'd add serpents to his calligraphy monogram.

The rough, scaly texture of a gator's coat of armor scratched Kendell's arm. The creature gave her an appraising stare as it took up its position at her side. The look was the same Sanguine often had just before cutting to shreds one of Kendell's plans.

Though Colin had his snakes and his iron cane, Sanguine didn't look as if she'd been harmed. Assuming the serpent that had guided Myles to the puppies had been the swamp witch's doing, the devil had even less power than he thought.

Kendell stepped into the moonlight cast through the opening overhead. "Let her go. You've lost."

Snakes coiled around Kendell's feet before she heard Sanguine mutter under her breath, "Damn you. I had this under control."

The slithery creatures worked up Kendell's legs like compression socks with raw elastic tops. "Get them off me!" Her fear was getting the better of her.

Colin turned his back on Sanguine and faced his new play toy. "You can't imagine how long I've waited to have you at my mercy." The second alligator joined his companion at Colin's side. "The swamp witch and I were just having a little tug-of-war over who could control more creatures. Thanks to your interference, I guess I've won."

Sanguine let out a yelp of pain while the snakes around Kendell's feet tightened their grip. Kendell knew she'd made a mess out of Sanguine's plan, but it wasn't as if the young woman had bothered sharing her ideas.

"You're never getting out of this hell," Kendell said. "You must know that. We'll never give in to you."

"Yes, yes, and next you'll tell me you're not alone. What you're not getting is that I welcome you to my hell. How else am I to learn how to use my new powers if there aren't people to control? I can hardly be a god in life if I don't first learn what that means."

"You did all this just to trap me, didn't you?" Kendell asked.

He walked slowly around her as though appraising a whore for his brothel. "You've proven to be a challenge. I find so few truly worthy opponents."

"Then let Sanguine go. She's just a distraction."

Colin gave a flick of his hand, and the snakes that bound Sanguine slithered away. Kendell knew her friend's natural instinct was to stay and fight, but not all battles were won on the front line. With a quick nod toward the door, Kendell hoped Sanguine would figure out that she wasn't alone.

MYLES KNEW he was greatly outnumbered by his own allies. Every female—human and canine—wanted to rush into the warehouse in some foolhardy attempt to save the women. The debate had grown from frustrating to tiresome.

"We have to leave this to Kendell, but there is a last-resort plan. I can funnel all our energy into her."

Sanguine took his arm. "Could you do the same for me? I nearly had control of all of Colin's little pets. With enough spiritual power, I could turn them all to our side. Once those snakes let go of Kendell, all Colin would have is his metal cane. At that point, the dogs could rush in and save her. What good would funneling our energy into Kendell do, really? She and Colin aren't engaged in some philosophical debate."

Polly had been occupied cleaning and dressing the scar on Muffin Top's jaw. "She's right. We don't need some spiritual-whirlwind disembodied fight between those two. Kendell needs to get out of there so we can finish up the seven gates and get our asses back to reality. Powering her up only gives Colin the playmate he's always wanted."

Myles was well aware of Colin's interest in Kendell. "Funneling all our energy into Sanguine is a bigger risk. Kendell and I have experienced the *deep waters* together. I know her in ways that transcend life. There's a reason we kept this option as a last resort. Don't forget, we're in hell. If my attempt at uniting us all goes wrong, we could be trapped here forever—especially considering the nonexistence of time in this realm."

Sanguine held his hand. "I trust you."

Polly gave Muffin Top back to Cheesecake and sat next to Sanguine. "I trust you too."

One by one, the remaining members of the band joined the circle and professed their belief in Myles and his abilities. Losing his sense of self came easily enough, but doing it with five open-minded women bordered on a sexual experience. Myles tried hard to keep that aspect of the experience out of his imagination. He gathered the band members as though forming a bouquet of flowers.

Lynn's spirit was soft, kind, and playful, with an innocence that couldn't be faked. Much as she might want to be the opposite of Lynn, Polly's firm resolve was a shield to protect her inner child, and she understood the keyboard player all too well. In his mind, Minerva stood bare for his inspection. Unafraid and unapologetic, the woman raised by hippies wouldn't turn away from any self-realization, even her attraction to her fellow rhythm-section bandmate. For all of her brashness, Scraper was the hardest to read. The tough, anti-feminine image she presented to the world was only a game she played while she figured out who she truly wanted to be.

To each woman, Myles presented his truest self—a misunderstood daydreamer desperate for acceptance but wary of people's assumptions. Though Kendell united them all and was his heart's desire, Myles turned the inner mirror that directed their spiritual laser beam toward Sanguine.

The swamp witch wasn't as open as the rest. He understood. After being alone for so much of her life, trusting others didn't come naturally for her. The band members had each other, and though Myles wasn't a part of the music, they accepted him as if he were. *We're not taking anything from you, but you must open your spirit for us to become a part of you.* He hoped she would understand.

Begrudgingly, she allowed him a glimpse of the curious little girl who wanted to spend all her time in the swamp with her friends, the animals. People frightened her and still did. Letting anyone close, as she had with Kendell, brought a calculated risk to her independence. Every human connection was one more step away from her beloved bayou.

With the mutual baring of souls completed, Myles felt Sanguine turn her attention to every animal in the vicinity —from the two massive gators all the way down to the dozen mosquitoes that were hatching out of the stagnant water in a fifty-five-gallon drum behind the warehouse. She wasn't calling to them but seeing life through their eyes. The bloodsuckers had a yearning tempered by caution— instinct combined with stealth. The snakes, of which there were far more than Myles had imagined, reacted with aggression to any stimulation, positive or negative. They displayed a need to survive and distrusted all living things, including themselves. On and on the catalogue of animal helpers went until he had an understanding of Sanguine that went far beyond that of any of the women he offered her as helpers.

The four animals Sanguine didn't connect to were Cheesecake and her pups. With his senses at a distance, Myles only dimly noticed the dogs heading off for their part in the rescue. Much more noticeable were the two canebrake rattlesnakes. At five feet long, they had wrapped around Kendell's legs and were squeezing her warmth into their cold-blooded bodies. Sanguine didn't command them as Myles had expected. Instead, each picked up the aroma of a longed-for squirrel. They eased out of the pant legs of Kendell's jeans. Being so close, Myles considered trying to get a message to her, but he feared the idea of a snake hissing out his message might have unwelcome consequences later on for their love life.

From the snake's awareness, he felt her shake her foot to remove the final coil. The serpent nearly lost control and bit her, but Sanguine persuaded the creature that more enticing prey lay elsewhere. As the two slithered toward the shadows, he got a fleeting impression of the squirrel Sanguine had tempted into the warehouse.

Had there only been the two snakes, Myles was certain Sanguine would have sent them after Colin, but for every animal she could entice, he would control three more. Her gentle nature with wild creatures was no match for his authoritarian commands.

With the snakes safely pursuing their dinner, Sanguine turned the gang's attention to her two favorite gators. The lazy creatures liked thinking they were in charge of any domain they inhabited. The monsters, though, were merely Sanguine's eyes.

From the open loading-bay door, four fearsome creatures entered like a well-trained military squad. The much larger leader took her command position in front of Kendell while the three attack commandoes formed a skirmish line in front of Colin. From the gator's perspective, the animals were far too energetic, but warm-blooded creatures had a habit of working too hard.

The alligators lingered by the open door as the woman morsel was escorted out by the strange dogs, who must have wanted to save their meal for later.

15

---

*S*anguine knew where the final two gates needed to be, just as she knew who had to guard them. Letting the others discuss their ideas was a distraction, but one that proved useful in not opening a debate.

As everyone climbed back in the VW, she took Kendell by the hand. "It's down to the two of us. Like Delphine said, we're the two halves of the cage. You have to provide the seventh gate, and I the sixth. There's no other choice. My grandmother's hell isn't nearly as secure as she led me to believe. With these gates, you and I can be more proactive at containing Colin. Much as I admire my grandmother, being here in the hell she created, I can see how naïve she was to think Colin would just accept his banishment."

Much to Sanguine's relief, Kendell was becoming more amenable to her ideas. "Your grandmother's old shack out in the swamp wouldn't be the worst place for a gate. Even though Colin's been there before, it's not the easiest spot to get to."

Before Sanguine got in the van, she called to Minerva in the driver's seat. "Head out to Highway 55."

With everyone saddled up, Cheesecake stood a good six feet from the door. At first, Kendell tried to entice her into the bus, but the she-wolf wasn't having it.

"It's okay, girl. You and your pups keep an eye on Colin. Just don't get caught. We'll be back to find you as soon as we can."

Sanguine was never sure how much of Kendell's ramblings the dog understood. The animal gave Kendell a slight nod before trotting off toward the river.

Polly jumped out of the van. "I'm going with her. You don't need me out in the swamp. I'd just be bitching about the demonic mosquitoes."

Lynn jumped out too. "I was hoping someone would give me an excuse."

No great loss. Sanguine kept the thought to herself. At least Minerva and Scraper, who remained in their seats up front, looked like they could handle themselves in a fight.

Kendell, who tended to humor her bandmates, said, "Okay. Just be careful. Colin's a wily devil. Once we're done in the swamp, we'll be headed for Scratch and Sniff. It only makes sense to make that the last gate. Delphine can be my lookout. If you manage to contain Colin in his penthouse, we can meet up at the shop. If not, we'll find you once we're done."

Polly gave a quick "Sounds good" before breaking into a

run to keep up with Cheesecake and her puppies, who were already half a block ahead.

Sanguine moved from the crowded back seat to the empty middle bench. "I left a canoe hidden in the reeds, but it will only carry three of us."

Even with her rough exterior, Scraper didn't appear to be the swamp type of woman. Fortunately, she volunteered to stand guard at the bus. "I don't imagine Colin will escape the four hell beasts, not to mention our fellow harpies, but I for one am done with surprises. From here on, we watch our backs."

It wasn't the worst idea Sanguine had heard lately.

She suppressed her enjoyment of the ride out to her grandmother's swamp. The old VW had character, as though it ran as much on magic as gasoline. But Sanguine resisted being seduced by such conveniences, which had a way of dulling her edge, especially in hell.

Then there was the swamp. After her parents' mysterious death when she was just a child, the waterways, marshes, and cypress groves had become her home. Her grandmother had sent her to boarding school, but that was mostly to pacify the state's requirements since there was no school bus that ran out to the bayou. The education put her far ahead of the other families who called rural Louisiana home—such things as state laws weren't given much attention by people who lived off the land. But with every vacation and summer break, the swamp became her true home.

The trip gave her too much time to think. The others

carried on their mindless prattle. She could filter out the useless information—the lovebirds in the back and the band members who didn't want to admit their attraction for each other up front.

And up ahead was her grandmother's old cabin. The woman knew more than any person Sanguine had ever met, yet all she wanted was to be left in peace. *Stupid voodoo curse.*

Rocks hit the underside of the VW as it rolled into the turnout used in life by the crawfish trappers and fishermen to launch their boats. Of course, such people didn't exist in her grandmother's version of reality.

Sanguine was first out of the vehicle. The fear of what traps her grandmother might have left behind mixed with excitement at being home and made her hurry to the hidden blind that housed her canoe.

Kendell and Myles were saying their goodbyes to the women who would stand guard. *Like there's anything they can do if danger does strike.* Sanguine would have been happier if Myles had stayed behind as well, but some battles weren't worth the energy. She needed Kendell to perform her little voodoo ritual, and if she insisted on bringing her burly man with her, well, Sanguine would just have to live with it.

Neither of the city dwellers looked comfortable in the narrow boat. It took a fair bit of balancing to prevent them from tipping it over. Sanguine jumped into the back and shifted her weight to use the momentum to move the canoe away from shore. "Just try to match each other's paddling. This isn't a race. I'll balance out the difference back here while steering. Don't get distracted."

People—city folk—had a nasty habit of sightseeing while out in the bayou. Usually that meant more talking than paddling. Sanguine didn't have the time or patience for such nonsense. As they worked deeper into the bayou and away from the road, she noticed her grandmother had built the alternate-reality swamp she'd long talked about. The invasive water hyacinths that choked every tributary were gone. The waterways looked like veins in a leaf as they cut through the countless marsh islands. She looked over the side to see if her grandmother had included wildlife in her created oasis. A water moccasin was undulating next to the boat. "Run ahead and tell her we're coming."

The black snake doubled its speed and shot ahead of the boat.

Kendell once again splashed water into the boat as she tried to turn in her seat. "What was that about?"

"A little welcoming party from my grandmother. I don't want to stumble into any of her traps, so I thought the little critter might smooth the way."

Kendell put the oar across the sides of the boat and turned fully back to Sanguine. "You expect to see her out here?"

"I don't expect anything. But this hell needs a central command post. There's a consciousness to everything that we've encountered."

The girl's movements were destabilizing the boat. "You don't think that was just Colin?"

This is how people get hurt out here—by not paying attention.

"Colin's an amateur. Do you really think Cheesecake would

have ended up with puppies if he'd been in charge? Someone has been observing everything that's going on."

"And they speak dog?"

The sarcasm almost made Sanguine tell Kendell to get back to rowing. "Any good swamp witch worth her gumbo filé knows what animals are thinking. We've still got some river ahead of us, and with it all cleaned up like this, I need to focus on where we're going."

At least Kendell didn't need to be told twice.

The perpetual darkness of night was pierced by a ray of light like the sun shining through a gap in the clouds onto the island. The colors sparkled like jewels in the dark setting of the swamp at night.

Sanguine paddled with renewed vigor from the hope of seeing her grandmother again. Rather than work around the shore, she beached the boat opposite the cypress grove.

"This is where we get out. Let me take the lead. My grandmother was never fond of strangers and had her little tricks to keep them at bay." After getting out of the boat, Sanguine put her hands on her hips and stretched out her back. The trip wasn't long, but it was arduous. The sun felt good on her face. She couldn't even estimate how long they'd been putting their plan in place in the forever night. "We'll cut over the top of the island. My grandmother's cabin is in the trees on the other side."

Once they'd climbed the short rise from the shore, the true nature of the island became apparent. It wasn't just the swamp that had been cleaned up. In place of the scrub forest were lush vegetable and herb gardens—every plant a swamp witch would need to cast her spells. But what most caught Sanguine's attention was the cabin perched at the top of the knoll. Instead of a weather-beaten shack that hung in the tree limbs like a giant bird's nest, the house gleamed in fresh yellow and white paint and sat on the ground like any normal dwelling. "I've only seen her cabin in the trees. This must be a version of her reality that predates the storm that lifted the cabin off the ground."

Rabbits frolicked in the vegetation, but on a closer look, Sanguine realized these weren't the fluffy bunnies her grandmother had let her keep as pets as a child. With their fangs, razor-sharp teeth, and red eyes, they looked more like protective guardians. "So that's why you guys haven't eaten all the vegetables. You look more like carnivores."

The smell of freshly made alligator boudin made Sanguine break into a full run. "Grandma!"

The woman who stepped out of the house was much younger and prettier than Sanguine remembered. Even her blue-white eyes were sparkling sea-blue and clear, no longer blind. But the smile let Sanguine know this vibrant woman was indeed the old woman who'd raised her. "I've been expecting you, my dear."

Sanguine hugged her so tightly she feared she might harm her, but this wasn't the frail body she remembered. "I've missed you so much."

"Come inside, everyone. I've got lunch ready."

It wasn't like Sanguine to let loose with her emotions in front of others. She quickly recovered her composure. "Do you know why we're here?"

The inside of the cabin was as much of a surprise as the outside. The old, beat-up furniture looked brand-new. "I know everything that goes on in my realm. It's a part of me." She turned to Kendell and Myles. "Delphine did a better job than I expected. You two came as quite the surprise."

Sanguine couldn't stand sentimentality for long, even when it came to her grandmother. "What about the gates, Grandma? Will they do any good, or are we wasting our time?"

Sanguine's grandmother wasn't the type to mince words, so she got right to the point. "They aren't the worst idea. By consolidating his access into seven points, Colin is given a maze to work through instead of pushing randomly at the edges of my reality. I've never rejected the ideas of voodoo, so I'll accept this Guinee-based model."

Sanguine feared crossing her lifelong mentor. "I need to be one of the gatekeepers. You're in charge of this realm, so you can't do it, but I can act in your place. I'll only accept the position, though, if you agree."

"It's time for you to step out of my shadow. You're the swamp witch now. You and Kendell are in charge of this hell. I only created it."

As Sanguine feared, Kendell didn't react well to the news of being co-manager of hell. "What? No one said anything about me being in charge of this place. I'll be the final gatekeeper, but I don't know anything about what you've built."

"I'm sure Delphine told you that you and Sanguine are the two halves of the cage. What did you think she meant?"

"But once we set up the gates, I'm free to leave, right? I

can go on with my life?" Kendell sounded as though she was trying to get out of a homework assignment.

Sanguine's grandmother refilled Kendell's glass of sweet tea. "No one's stopping you. If Sanguine is to be the next gatekeeper, I assume you'll be in charge of number seven. You'll have plenty of notice should Colin attempt to leave."

"Assuming he sticks to using the gates," Myles said. "What if he tries a prison break?"

"The gates aren't just a means for him to prove he's worthy," the old swamp witch said. "They're also windows into this world for the guardians. Kendell and Sanguine now have multiple images of what's happening in this world. Think of them as being like prison guard towers." Sanguine's grandmother had a way making the confusing easy to understand.

"That still doesn't stop him from looking for some weakness to exploit," Myles said, making Sanguine wonder if he ever listened to his elders. "He's gained quite a bit of knowledge about his prison cell. Given enough time, which doesn't seem to be an issue here, he'll figure out how to turn every bit of power to his advantage."

"And you think that's unintentional on my part? Baron Malveaux, Lincoln Laroque, and now the combination known as Colin Malveaux all share the same evils—unbridled greed and lust for power. By giving him room to roam, I give him false hope, and then I pull the rug out from under him. The simple lessons of humility learned from failures are lost on Colin. I intend to educate him."

"Sounds like you're trying to rehabilitate a water

moccasin. Snakes don't change. They strike when least expected."

Sanguine had heard enough. "No one understands the nature of animals better than a Wiccan witch."

~

KENDELL COULDN'T GET out of the swamp fast enough. She was a city girl, and any time away from her natural environment made her jumpy. The old swamp witch's reimagined cabin was nice. It reminded Kendell of a less palatial version Mary's plantation on the Westbank. But being surrounded by mystical gators, snakes, and deadly bunnies wasn't her idea of a pleasant afternoon, especially after her run-in with Colin. If she never saw another snake in her life, that'd be just fine. She rubbed her legs at the memory of the slick creatures coiled menacingly inside her jeans. The sixth gate was secure, and that was what mattered.

Myles leaned forward from his perch in the middle of the boat. "So Delphine's next? Are you sure that's the best place? You can still change your mind."

She didn't see how. "If Baron Samedi is right and I can download this curse into the guitar pick like some spiritual memory stick, it'll be worth it."

"You won't miss it?"

It had been a gift from the loas of the dead. She'd played some killer music with the magical pick, but in the end, it was just another enhancement. "I think it's time I learned to play without magic."

"You won't get an argument from me. I just wanted to be sure. I am still a little confused about using Scratch and Sniff, though."

Kendell was relieved he hadn't said *I told you so.* "It's where Delphine connected me to the curse. Before that I was just dabbling in voodoo and magic. Besides, it makes the most sense to return the voodoo totem to its natural home."

She knew he'd never trust Delphine—and for good reason.

"And you don't think she'll just return it to Colin like last time?"

"It's not hers to return. Giving her the totem was a mistake—maybe my biggest mistake. But honestly, I'm not sure the totem that we know will show up in her shop. What I pulled from the floor in Colin's office wasn't from this reality. It's still intangible. We can only handle it with the guitar pick attached. It's from our world but is locked in this one."

He returned to his paddling. The closer they came to the VW, the darker the swamp became.

Scraper stood watch on the jetty as the canoe rounded the final bend in the river. "About time you guys showed up. That VW is versatile, but it's no swamp buggy. Did you get what you were after?"

Kendell was the first one out of the boat. "The old swamp witch will keep an eye out for Colin and let Sanguine know if he's approaching. I'm not sure she was being completely open about the level of threat. Maybe she's just a little overly confident in her creation. She'll help, and that's what we were after. Anything interesting happen while we were gone?" With Colin safely thirty miles away, she assumed the wait had been more boring than scary.

Minerva walked over from the water's edge. "We took the time to evaluate the area's animals. They weren't all united in protecting us."

Sanguine sounded perplexed. "What are you talking about? The animals out here are my grandmother's sentinels."

"Well then, she's not the only one who has figured out how to use them. Nearly all of the animals stood guard over us. From the gators to the cockroaches, it was clear which creatures were on our side. But the bats and crawfish staged multiple coordinated attacks on the jetty's defenses. I don't think they were trying to attack us as much as get into the bayou."

Kendell stared out toward the dark water. "How could you tell? It's so dark. I wouldn't see a crawfish until it crawled up my leg or a bat until it landed in my hair."

"Watch long enough, and you'll see the battles. We first noticed when the water started churning around the inlet. River gars started thrashing against the flow as if they were trying to jump out of the water. Then we saw the bats coming down in formation. It only lasted a few minutes, but the battle was clearly to the death. We started taking notes on every creature we could find."

As usual, Myles took the least positive position on hell's stability. "So the old swamp witch uses animals to keep an eye on us, and presumably Colin, but we already know he's figured out how to control at least some of the creatures. He's really pushing at every weakness he can find."

The longer they sat around, the more time Myles would have to develop his pessimism. Kendell needed to get everyone moving. "We're down to the final gate. Then we perform the ceremony to unite them. We're so close."

Minerva pulled out her keys. "I'll have us back to the city in no time." She started laughing at her unintentional joke.

Sanguine turned back to her canoe. "For the ceremony to work, each guardian will have to be at their gate. It'd be silly for me to ride all the way into town just to have someone bring me back."

Kendell agreed. "We'll come back as soon as the ceremony is complete." On the trip back to town, she snuggled close to Myles in the back seat. "Do you really think this has all been a wasted effort?"

"If we accomplish nothing other than getting Baron Samedi his cane and getting him back to Guinee, we'll have closed off the most obvious escape route for Colin. As for strengthening the walls of this hell, I guess I understand voodoo better than Wicca. But since we know the two beliefs don't mix well, it sounds like trying to put an oil-based paint on top of a water-based primer."

Though she wasn't big on home repair, it didn't take much to understand that oil and water didn't mix. "You're afraid our fix will start peeling off the walls?"

He leaned back and put his feet on the back of the bench seat in front of them. "We're buying some time. Right now, I'll take every minute we can get. But once we're home, I don't intend to take for granted that this problem is solved. Not yet anyway."

She nodded as she lay against his chest. "Always a sound course of action."

Sleep wasn't a state she'd experienced since making the wild ride to hell, but lying against his chest gave her a similar sense of peace. The drive back to the Quarter was the most rest she'd had since leaving their apartment, which seemed like a lifetime ago.

As Minerva took the Tchoupitoulas exit, Kendell yelled from the back seat, "We need to go to the bank first. I'll need the totem and my golden pick. It'll also give us a chance to catch up on what's going on without wasting much time."

Kendell couldn't stop smiling when they reached the bank and she saw Cheesecake standing guard out front. She pulled the sliding door open as fast as she could. "How's my girl doing?"

The she-wolf nearly knocked Kendell on her butt.

"Easy, girl. You still don't realize your size."

But Cheesecake wasn't going to let a good reunion go without lots of kisses, even if a wolf's tongue was considerably larger and more powerful than a Lhasa apso's.

Kendell gave the short-haired ears the rubs that always made Cheesecake whimper. "I missed you too, but we've still got work to do. Since you're here, I hope that means your pups are doing okay. We're all going to be reunited very soon."

Myles was standing at the large entry doors. "And the sooner we get the totem, the sooner we can be done."

She knew he was right, but letting go of her dog was

never easy. "I'll be as fast as I can, girl. Keep up the great work. There's a whole bag of treats waiting for you and your pups when we get home."

She could feel the change in dimension as they ran through the old building. Like goose bumps that came out of nowhere or static electricity that made her hair stand on end, it was easy to miss, but once noticed, it was unmistakable.

The door to the office stood open. Baron Samedi sat at the desk, but the two Malveaux children weren't to be seen.

Kendell walked up to the voodoo totem that sat at the middle of the desk. "I'm ready."

Baron Samedi handed her his cane. "Put the silver skull against your chest and the end of the cane on the golden pick atop the totem. Imagine your soul free of the curse."

She couldn't believe that was all there was to it. It had taken ten days to become a part of the curse, and that time had been literally gut-wrenching. "And what will you do?"

"The curse doesn't want to live inside a person. It's pure energy. You are also made of energy. The two don't mix. The cane helps you expel the curse like letting blood out of your veins. At first you might feel some discomfort, but soon you'll feel the relief of letting go."

He made it sound like a vampire seducing his victim, which didn't give her comfort. She took the cane and put the skull to her heart. "Let's just get it over with."

Myles guided the end to the golden triangle. "If anything goes wonky, I'm pulling this away."

She nodded and let him proceed. Rather than the cane entering her chest, she felt her heart moving toward the knob. It felt as though miniature slivers of metal had lodged in her chest and the cane was the magnet pulling them out. Baron Samedi had a sadistic definition of *discomfort*, but painful as the experience was, Kendell remained conscious. She felt Myles tug on the cane, but she shook her head. It was working. There was a light in her heart that had been missing since the day she'd first learned of her connection to Baron Malveaux.

With the last shard of the curse removed, Kendell breathed a little easier. She continued to press the skull against her chest. Anything left behind could too easily regenerate within her. But the evil and desire for vengeance had left.

When the cane became nothing more than a stick with a fancy headpiece, she tossed it aside. "What happens now?"

Baron Samedi took back his cane. "Your connection now fully resides in the golden pick. You are the only one who can access it. Think about Colin, or anyone who's been affected by the curse, and you'll receive the information you desire."

"But the curse itself still exists?"

He tapped the cane against the floor. "All Delphine did was give you control over it. With that command isolated in the pick, and the pick residing in an in-between dimension, no one else can access it. The spell is dormant, but that doesn't mean it's dead."

Kendell knew that was the best she could expect. "And what if Colin manages to make it through the other six gates? Will he gain control over the curse?"

"With you as guardian, he'll have to face the challenge of

self-sacrifice," Baron Samedi said. "Someone in his position wouldn't even understand the meaning of the word. Though the totem and pick will look like a trap should he answer wrong, the reality is he'll have to voluntarily return to the totem with the curse hanging over his head to complete his mission. He'll have to embrace the judgment for his wrongdoings."

Myles tapped his foot nervously against the desk. "Wouldn't that just put him back where we started?"

"Baron Malveaux has lived out his life. Lincoln Laroque accepted the same fate when he ingested the baron and the two beings became one. Their only path forward is to accept death, pass through Guinee, and join the *deep waters*. By entering the totem, he will begin that process. Though it's the seventh gate between this hell and your reality, since he's dead in that realm, it's actually a one-way ticket to Guinee. By accepting his fate, he will be agreeing to the rules of Guinee."

Myles didn't look completely pacified by the answer. "Sanguine talked about consolidating the Malveaux and Laroque greed into one person and then removing that soul from humanity as a way of purifying us all. Was that just bullshit?"

"Human souls are joined together. One cannot be removed, only isolated for a time. By using that time to rehabilitate the individual before returning him to the *deep waters*, all humanity learns the lesson of a single redemption. Evil isn't to be removed—it's to be overcome. All life is about the learning."

Kendell was trying to get used to handling the totem. As

it had no mass, she had to rely on the guitar pick, but having her hand disappear into the wooden sculpture decorated with nails and rough-sewn leather made her feel as though she was putting her hand in the mouth of the beast. "Let's get over to Scratch and Sniff so I can be done with this thing."

Back out on the street, Myles helped her into the van. "We're almost finished."

She turned to Cheesecake, who kept faithful watch at the front door of the bank. "I'll be back to get you just as soon as the ceremony is complete."

As they pulled up to Delphine's shop, she could feel Myles's anxiety grow. He'd been held prisoner in the shop, tormented by flames, like a witch burning at the stake.

"You don't have to come in," she said. "I need to contact Delphine to make sure we can use her shop, but once that's done, I'll just make the veve and we can get out of here."

"No. If it's a trap, it would be better for me to spring it. Even with the dogs, Polly, and Lynn keeping an eye on him, I don't trust that Colin didn't hide some other booby trap where we wouldn't expect it. The best place to catch an adversary is somewhere they think they've already made safe."

She hated to admit it, but his reasoning made sense. "We'll be ready to come save you should your paranoia prove to be right."

He gave her a kiss before exiting the bus. "Right back at ya."

She wasn't crazy about him entering the shop alone. He cautiously pushed the door open and, to her relief, nothing came jumping out after him, but she walked up the stairs to the front porch just to be close. Though they hadn't been long in the swamp, her eyes had lost the sharp night vision that had developed from spending so much time in the late evening.

"What do you see?" she asked.

"It's as I left it. Apparently, those fire wraiths only scorch walls if time is moving. It smells a bit of burned sulfur, but otherwise, everything looks okay. Give me a minute to check out the back voodoo library."

He disappeared behind the black drape that separated the perfume retail store from the back office and hidden alcove filled with voodoo journals.

Each moment he was out of sight made her think it was time to rush in with curses blazing. When the curtains finally parted, she was ready for battle. She looked him up and down as thoroughly as she could in the dim light before letting down her guard. "How was it?"

"The place is a wreck. He cleared out about a quarter of the books. Totems are scattered on the floor. I'm guessing he was searching for anything he could let loose but still control. What he couldn't use, he tossed on the floor like a petulant child. Nothing attacked me, though."

Kendell turned to the others. "You two keep watch out here with Myles. Colin is a hell of a lot closer here than when we were in the swamp."

It wasn't that she wanted to be alone in the creepy shop, but people and canines had been putting themselves at risk for long enough. She searched among the wreckage left by hurricane Colin. For someone with limited resources, he didn't seem to appreciate what he had. Even if he couldn't read the books or control the spirits, leaving them tossed around the floor like a toddler's toys appeared careless in the extreme. She picked up the first totem and set it back in the display case. There had to be something that would connect her to Delphine. It would be something obvious. As she arranged the books back on the shelves and the wooden sculptures back into the case, she noticed every item, when positioned properly, was facing Delphine's throne.

Of course, she never performed any magic without first getting comfortable in her chair. Kendell lowered herself onto the throne. She felt like a little kid pretending to be a grown-up by sitting in her father's favorite chair. "If you're listening, I need to talk to you."

The silence was deafening. Sitting in the voodoo priestess's chair, Kendell realized the problem. She'd been relying on others to do the magic for her. First it was Myles and his psychometric skills of reading past energy in items. Then she'd ridden him like a horse into Guinee and the *deep waters.* Delphine had taught her well, but Kendell still hung onto her like a child who was too scared to enter kindergarten on her own.

She set the voodoo totem on the table. *I can do this.*

Using what Myles had taught her, Kendell cleared her mind of all thoughts. Every bit of magic she'd encountered first required the practitioner to acquire a Zen-like awareness of self and others. Physical space was little more than a representation of spiritual connections. Being in Delphine's shop was Kendell's way of acknowledging their connection. Sitting in the priestess's chair would prove she was no longer the student.

When she opened her eyes, she saw Delphine shimmering in the light of another dimension as she sat in the chair opposite her. "Very good. Now that you've conjured me, what do you want?"

Delphine always chose her words carefully. The question wasn't whether Kendell sought her help, but what Kendell hoped to achieve.

"I'm taking the Wiccan equivalent of Baron Samedi's position as the final gatekeeper. Should Colin learn enough to pass the other six gates, I'll hold the key to him rejoining humanity or being cast into a hell only I can open."

"Yes, but what do you *want*?"

Kendell wasn't completely sure she knew the answer. "I want to love others without putting them in danger. Life shouldn't be about constantly coming to people's rescue or hoping to be saved by someone I love. Colin and the curse have been like evil shadows that threaten everyone I care about."

"And by being the seventh guardian, you believe you'll be free of that menace?"

She couldn't imagine what it would feel like to no longer be looking over her shoulder in fear. "It would isolate him to one window of my life, and for the most part, I could keep that drape closed."

"You consider me the drape in this scenario?"

Kendell had never been a fan of Myles's skepticism regarding Delphine, but the voodoo queen wasn't blameless when it came to the challenges Kendell faced. "You do bear more than a little responsibility regarding the curse, Colin Malveaux, and my connection."

"I'll agree to letting you use my shop as your seventh gate. You can rely on me to contact you should he approach my shop in his hell. But as I told you from the beginning, my primary responsibility is to the legacy of Marie Laveau. That doesn't change."

With all of the alterations since Marie had first cast the curse, Delphine's stipulation of honoring her ancestor sounded like a get-out-of-jail-free card for the voodoo madam, but having her stand between Colin's hell and Kendell's reality would at least provide the buffer Kendell needed to get on with her life. "I can accept that."

Delphine fondled the black stone that hung from her necklace. "Have you given any thought to how you'll get home after this adventure? It sounds like you might be getting close to the end."

Accepting responsibility for her magic wasn't going to be easy. "I guess we can't exactly drive over the bridge at high speed like last time. The cane and silver skull performed perfectly in connecting the two realities, but now that they're fused together, that's not going to work for our return. Between the seven of us, four dogs, and help from other dimensions, I can open all seven gates from hell to life. But as gatekeepers, I'm not sure we can hold them open and pass through at the same time."

"Then you have nothing. Guess I'll have to get to work."

Kendell never liked being patronized, and Delphine's dismissive attitude made her want to discuss a plan she hadn't been sure about. "An idea keeps occurring to me. The second line to a burial is always somber, but the one leaving the dead and returning to life is always upbeat. I can envision a second line out of hell, but I'd need people on that side to pull it off. Objects are just things. People and love are what really save our souls."

16

*K*endell had been dreading the next step of the plan. She squeezed Myles so tightly she wondered why their two bodies didn't fuse into one. "This is when things get scary."

He was never the first to let go of an embrace. His arms around her felt like home. "You can do it. Minerva and Scraper are rounding up Polly and Lynn. They will bring Cheesecake here. Then I can escort the band to the Scratchy Dog. We'll have each other's backs, but for good measure, Doughnut Hole will be with me. Cheesecake will stand guard over you. And Muffin Top and Cupcake can watch over Miss Fleur in the convent and Mary across the river. Baron Samedi will be with Serephine and Antoine. Sanguine is far enough away that Colin can't reach her. We won't be as exposed as he might think."

The plan was sound, but that didn't relieve her

apprehension. She only felt safe expressing her fears in his arms. "That doesn't prevent him from trying."

He caressed her back the way she did Cheesecake's when she was afraid. "We can't plan for every possible attack."

Reluctantly, Kendell pulled out of his arms. "And the longer we give him, the more chance he has to plan another assault."

"Everything's in place. Minerva will be back any minute. Once we have the ceremony behind us, we'll have accomplished our main goal."

She'd been careful not to think about home. The distraction of fixating on the finish line had tripped her up more than once. But thoughts of their new apartment, the coffee shop, and playing before an audience again beckoned her onward. "Thanks for believing in me."

"You started it."

He always had a way of making her smile.

She heard the underpowered engine of the VW from a block away. "Time to do this thing."

Though she hated that Myles would be leaving her, seeing Cheesecake's smiling face, which took up the entire passenger side of the windshield, lightened her mood considerably. She pulled away from Myles and opened the bus door. The wolf jumped out of the van but did a quick reconnaissance of the area before returning for her well-deserved hugs.

"You are such a good girl. I know you'll protect me." As strong as the bond was between her and Myles, nothing could compare to the loyalty between a woman and her dog.

~

COLIN KNEW the old bus was on its way to pick up the two meddlesome girls and their loathsome hellhounds long before he saw the dim headlights. The rickety sound of the pathetic engine could be heard from a mile away. He didn't even bother looking down at the reunion below. The bats overhead told him everything he needed to know. Lines of the dark-winged creatures spread across the city like information tentacles. Kendell's people weren't all in position yet, but it wouldn't be long. He'd only have one shot at disrupting her plan.

As the bus drove off, the sky that had been filled with flying rodents cleared to the ever-present night clouds. In the distance, dark lines radiated out from the bank toward the locations of his enemies. Baron Samedi's involvement was expected, as was the gang's tactical mistake of pulling in their defenses. He could feel what his eyes confirmed: they'd turned their attention away from him.

As the bats' formation moved two blocks away from his penthouse, Colin headed for the elevator. Though hell deprived him of time as he'd once understood it, events continued to progress. "No one understands a prison quite as well as an inmate."

He headed down Canal Street toward the river. For the entire time his realm had been invaded, he'd avoided the abandoned tower near the nonoperational ferry. It was time to call in the favor.

As he approached the World Trade Center, the front door opened on its own. From the outside, the building appeared to be little more than dark, cold concrete and glass, but as he crossed the threshold, overhead florescent lights announced his presence. Unlike every other embassy in hell, this one wasn't secluded in its private dimension.

Dust on the lock to the guardroom indicated it hadn't been touched. The blundering kids might have seen fit to ransack his offices, but they hadn't thought to check out the supposedly neutral repository for paranormal artifacts. Marie's journals had at least revealed a useful spell for resetting security systems. He punched in the code he'd created.

The guardroom sparked to life as he entered, but all he needed was the duffle bag filled with voodoo totems and journals he'd secured from Delphine's shop. The security-camera screens confirmed what he already knew. His bats were forming up along the paranormal energy lines that spread from the bank to the foolish kids' magical playhouses. So long as the bank with the trapped Baron Samedi was the main focus of the energy, he had time to act.

He picked up the phone and dialed 666. "I'm here. Let me up."

Out in the lobby, a light came on above the middle elevator. He left the guardroom and did his best to return the lock to its dusty, unused appearance. As he stepped into the ornate lift, he felt an inkling of his former self. This building had never relied on external electricity. Its design, meant to catch the power of passing storms, had enabled it to remain functional even in the make-believe world of the witch.

When the door opened, he didn't worry about the

formality of buzzing the only occupied office in the entire thirty-three-story structure. He pushed open the doors, expecting to see Luther Noire sitting at his desk. In spite of living out his hell alone, Colin was actually surprised the portly man wasn't where he belonged.

"This is no time for games." Luther might be a curmudgeon, but money trumped irascibility. The man could damn well show himself to his primary investor. "I'm losing my patience, Luther. You know why I'm here."

Instead of the man materializing like some apparition, his voice came across the intercom on the desk. "I told you, there aren't any artifacts that can make the leap from life to hell."

"Bullshit. Your little trinkets aren't even *in* the land of the living. We both know you've got a hidden dimension. New Orleans Bank and Trust has been funding your little experiment since before the War Between the States. I know. I was there. I'm calling in the loan."

"Now I'm calling bullshit. If it hadn't been for my predecessor, you would have never laid your hands on Samedi's cane. I'd say you made out pretty well on the deal."

Colin knew the voice over the intercom wouldn't sound so bold if Luther were there in person, but the argument from afar wasn't getting him anywhere, and he didn't have time for the debate. "See how well you do without me in the land of the living. Do you honestly believe my mother is going to continue this philanthropic activity without my influence?"

"Where, or when, the paranormal artifacts are stashed

isn't important. They're secured even from me. I can't help you."

Colin wasn't so easily dissuaded. "Fine. Give me the controls for the building."

The swamp witch portioned out power to Colin's high-rise like a parent worried about the utility bill. The World Trade Center, however, had a static charge that would rival the swamp witch's hurricane.

"Go up to the old restaurant on the roof," Luther said. "The controls that activate the rotation of the circular room also harness the building's power."

Colin hoisted the duffle bag over his shoulder like a dockworker and headed back to the elevator. A familiar feeling of smug satisfaction threatened to bring a smile to his face. He didn't actually want Luther's objects. He just needed to know they were in the building in some form.

The elevator opened to the expansive circular room. Though lower than his penthouse office, it still commanded an impressive view of the city. He hauled the bag to a conference table and carefully removed the contents. The time spent matching up each sculpture to the corresponding journal had been arduous. He never had been a great scholar. Deciphering Marie's codes had been one of the most painful mental experiences of his life, but that day's events would make the effort worth the struggle.

With the eight sculptures lining the table like a board of directors awaiting their orders, he proceeded to the journals. Each described the person imprisoned and the spell that had been used. Though he'd suffered the same fate, he couldn't care less about the first three-quarters of each journal. He flipped one journal at a time to the section about utilizing the trapped energy.

Though education had never interested him, understanding the fundamentals of power—be it economic, political, or electrical—had been the defining objective of his life. "Eight sculptures, and four arms to the building. The old swamp witch might be out to get me, but fate seems to be smiling on me."

The first challenge was getting four of the crudely carved heads out to the roof of the four projections of the building. He made notations of the four points of the compass on the journals so he'd remember which fetish went to which book. When the room started spinning, it would be hard to keep track of who was who out there.

The heavy sliding door probably hadn't been opened since Katrina. Once he had it separated from the sill, he forced his iron walking cane into the gap and pried the rusty hurricane-proof door open. Wind whipped around the building as if the old witch were trying to suck him up like Dorothy in *The Wizard of Oz*. "You don't dare kill me."

Though the tempest continued, he knew she'd never let him out of her realm. Death was an escape she'd denied him more than once. The wind might be an inconvenience, but it wasn't the threat she might have once imagined.

Just the same, he only took one sculpture out at a time. He might not get batted off the building, but dropping one of the totems would mean wasting valuable time retrieving it. When he had all four positioned at the building's edges, he returned to the comfort of the glassed-in room. The other four sculptures would have an easier time of it, sitting next to the windows and facing their brethren, but they would also be funneling far more energy through their delicate glass spirit jars. Whatever past sins had caused Marie to isolate the souls in the totems were about to be atoned for through electric and paranormal shock.

Colin consulted the eight ledgers and spoke the garbled words that had no meaning to him. Incantations might work to open the doorways to the totems, but that didn't mean he needed to understand how they worked.

The utility closet behind the stationary circular stage that took up the center of the old restaurant was more interesting. Though at one time the small control room had probably been little more than a bank of levers, Luther had made numerous modifications to direct the harnessed energy to his secret vaults. Being old-school, the man preferred manual controls to computers, which could so easily be hacked. The room reminded Colin of a locomotive's engineer cabin.

"Four arms, four banks of controls." The main levers reached from the center of the consoles to the floor. He pulled each up to the ceiling. They locked into their harnesses with loud thuds that shook the building. "That should change the direction of the power to the vaults to this room."

Next came the myriad of dials. To maintain the ideal environment that would keep the magical objects from overheating or in some way gaining strength, Luther had built an impressive array of controls. Colin turned each one to full strength.

Finally, he turned to the original 1960s console meant to

control the room's rotation. Using the energy stored up from the storm, he started spinning the circular room at the top of the building. Like a metaphysical turbine, the rotation drew power from the hidden objects and sent that energy to the voodoo fetishes in the room and then, in turn, out to their mates on the roof.

As his paranormal turbine came up to speed, he checked the flight pattern of his bats. Though the bank was still a part of their route, increasingly it was just another beacon and not the central hub.

He rushed back to Marie's journals. The final four incantations would open the totems on the roof and release their energy into the paranormal streams.

MYLES HAD NEVER HAD A DOG. Growing up, he'd always wanted one, but between changing schools every time his family moved and people thinking he was slightly crazy because of his psychometric abilities—or "daydreaming," as his parents described his flights of fantasy—the time had never been right. With Doughnut Hole at his side, he wondered if his life would have been far more normal if his parents had given in to his continuous requests.

Doughnut Hole put his front paws on the partition of the speakeasy as if he wanted to be Myles's first customer. "Not now, boy. I need to be ready for Kendell. Keep an eye out front. Me and the band are counting on you for protection."

The playful hellhound gave him a cheerful bark before heading to the front of the club.

With Doughnut Hole in place as guardian, Myles relaxed his mind to free his thoughts. He experienced the usual mad dash of ideas that shot off like fireworks no longer constrained in their tubes. Instead of following their directions, he imagined himself a kid lying on the grass, watching the display. Once the ideas played out, he grew peaceful in mind and spirit.

In his mind, he heard Kendell singing "Come Together." As she reached the chorus, the band in the next room joined in. He experienced the same light-headed bemusement he'd felt the first time he stepped into a house of mirrors. The guardians of all seven gates stared back at him as if they were his reflections. A giddy excitement swept through him, and as everyone started giggling, he realized the feeling wasn't his alone. Kendell nearly lost the lyrics, but then Polly and the girls covered for her as they always did for each other.

He felt Baron Samedi activate his end of the ceremony. Behind each of the guardians, another mirrorlike reality appeared. Though each person remained unchanged, the worlds they knew came into focus, taking the place of the dark-funhouse settings. Turning his back to look at his own life might break the spell, so Myles stayed still, but behind Kendell, he saw their apartment, Cheesecake, and even the black Lhasa apso puppy that would come to live with them. He nearly teared up to see Doughnut Hole as his true self again.

Myles remembered why he hated carnivals. In every

lovely reality that was home to each guardian, Colin Malveaux stepped out of the shadows like an evil clown intent on killing the merrymakers.

"Everyone remain at your gates." Myles knew enough about Malveaux's tricks to know when he was being conned. "He can't have passed by all of us."

"So you think he's trying to put us off our guard?" Polly asked.

Though Myles didn't always see eye to eye with Polly, he appreciated that she had a clear head in emergencies. "He's found a way to inject his presence into the formation of the gates. He wants us to believe we've already lost. He's bluffing."

Lynn gave in to her emotions. "How do you know? With all of us spread out, he might have stolen Baron Samedi's cane again. We could all be springing our own traps. I don't want to get stuck in hell forever. The doors are open. All we have to do is turn away from each other and jump through them. Even if it turns him loose, at least we'll be in our realities to combat him."

"No." Sanguine's voice echoed around the house of spiritual mirrors. "If any of us turns away, we'll all be lost. The seven gates only work if we're all in this together. No weak links."

"She's right," Kendell said. "The cage only works if all the bars are in place. Either we have him imprisoned, or we run the risk of him being in charge of us."

"Then what do we do?" Serephine's plaintive cry made everyone turn to her.

Mary calmed the child. "Be brave, little one. We're all in this together. You will never be alone."

Serephine's brother put his arm over her shoulders and pulled her close. "Father no longer has any power. Remember how he used to trick one of us into confessing to something we did by acting like the other one had already told him? This is just another of his stupid ruses."

The scared child's mother, Miss Fleur, was oddly quiet. Myles turned to her. "And what do you have to say? You knew a part of him better than any of us."

"He's cunning but not all that smart. Look again. He's not really in our realities."

Myles focused on the convent behind the old woman in drab attire. Colin Malveaux stood in the cloistered garden, but he looked like a cheap green-screen camera trick. The light that fell to the right of the plants and buildings illuminated him from the front. "He's still here, though. And none of us would dare make a move to go after him. If we close the gates now, we'll never be sure he hasn't planted a hidden way to sneak through our defenses."

Lynn, still panicking, said, "But with all of us here, who's going to save us?"

"We'll have to rely on the dogs. They saved us once. They can do it again." Scraper's calm voice reminded Myles of her bass playing: strong, confident, and unyielding.

Minerva, who always backed up her rhythm-section bandmate, said, "Everyone, call the pups."

Doughnut Hole and Cheesecake were the easiest to entice, but Cupcake and Muffin Top weren't far behind. Unfortunately, instead of the ferocious beasts everyone expected, Cheesecake appeared as her fluffy, lazy self and her puppies as the adorable balls of fur no one could resist.

Colin's sadistic laugh echoed from all of the mirror realities. "Those yappy dogs are the best you can throw at me? They're not even worth crushing with my cane."

The threat to Doughnut Hole nearly made Myles lose contact with the other guardians. "Touch one curly black hair on my puppy's head, and I'll end you once and for all."

"That goes for all the dogs," Kendell added.

Of course she was right, but the bond Myles felt for Doughnut Hole was overshadowing his connection to the other animals.

"The fact remains. You've got no person—or animal—to challenge me. I'm curious. What are you going to do next?"

If force of will had any impact, Colin would have found himself in dire circumstances. As it was, Myles was as curious as Colin. He could only think of one last being who didn't currently share their predicament. He looked into the mirror displaying Sanguine Delarosa. *Blood of the rose.*

She made eye contact and gave him a half nod of understanding. This was her grandmother's realm. If anyone could reach the old swamp witch while staying in contact with all the other guardians, it would be the one given the name of a true Wiccan descendant.

FROM SANGUINE'S earliest education in the mystical arts, she knew never to break a spiritual circle. She also knew reality did, in fact, play favorites. Only fools thought life was impartial. The time had passed for her grandmother to sit on the sidelines. She needed to take control of her creation.

Unfortunately, telepathy hadn't been Sanguine's strongest subject. Speaking over mental pathways seemed too much like ventriloquism, and she was never sure who was the bigger dummy.

Grandma, I need you.

The well-remembered face smiled from the shadows of the worn chair reflected in an inconspicuous mirror. The old woman at least had the good sense to show up as Sanguine remembered her and not at an age that would have made them look like sisters. Her blue-gray blind eyes never fooled Sanguine. The woman could see better than anyone. She just used her inner awareness of people. *What can I do for you, my dear one?*

Colin is on the loose. Sanguine had to keep her responses as short as possible to avoid moving her lips and giving the secret communication away.

Light sparkled in the old dead eyes like lightning flashing between the clouds. The comparison was driven home when Sanguine noticed the skies darkening, not only in the various mirrors but also the hell realm around her.

Colin stormed out of the shadows like a kid who'd had his toys taken away. "That's not fair. Time moves forward. You can't reconjure the hurricane."

Agnes Delarosa wasn't a witch to be trifled with. "I allowed time to move forward when you learned something. I had hoped that by having other people around, you might show some signs of remorse. Instead, you decided to play the devil. Not only have you learned nothing, but you've grown more callous as well. Like attracts like. The energy beams you've created by playing with your little paranormal Erector Set have called forth the energy of the storm. The old World Trade Center building might be impressive, but nothing stands in the way of a hurricane."

With all of the various window-mirrors into reality, it wasn't hard to make out the battle that raged around the high-rise. Bolts of electricity emanated from the voodoo totems, only to be met by lightning strikes from the hurricane that formed up around the structure. The storm's rotation made Sanguine dizzy, not because of its speed but because of its direction. *Time is moving backward.*

Sanguine turned to Kendell. "Quick, we need to finish the ceremony. We don't have much time."

The singer stretched out her arms. Her song sounded like it was being ripped from her heart. Everyone joined in just as the skies cleared.

"What the hell just happened?" Lynn asked.

"My grandmother turned time around to trap Colin in his realm. Once she turned the clock back a few minutes, Colin, the storm, and everything moved back beyond our reach."

"So is it over now?" Minerva asked. "Did we form the seven gates?"

Sanguine couldn't bring herself to be the one to break the circle. The band, however, had no such reservations. Rather than waiting for a verdict from someone who knew —namely Sanguine or Kendell—the girls split from the mirrors so fast it was as if they'd heard an ice cream truck.

Kendell was a little more respectful of their interdimensional guests. "Miss Fleur, Serephine, and Antoine, I want to thank you for your support. We couldn't have managed the seven gates without you. And Mary—"

"You don't even need to say it, dear. I will always be here for you no matter the dimension. Now, I suspect you have some work to do in order to find your way home. Please don't let me keep you. When you do return to your reality, you can be sure of a hot meal on my side of the river."

The sentimentality got to Kendell. "I love you all so very much."

$\mathcal{K}$endell sat on the steps of Scratch and Sniff, enjoying the afternoon sunlight on her face. From the stationary cloud formations that dotted the sky, she knew time was once again at a standstill, but at least it was daylight and no longer late evening.

Cheesecake had been the first to reach her. She sat watch next to Kendell. The wolf was panting. Her ears hung low as they did when the Lhasa apso version of herself was overly tired.

"We'll be home soon, girl. Then you and your puppies can have a nice long nap on the couch." She imagined how heavenly it would be to join them.

The bus with Myles, Doughnut Hole, and the band pulled up, and moments later, Kendell heard the yapping of Muffin Top from one end of the street and Cupcake from the other. Everyone—human and canine—looked drained.

Polly was first out of the sliding door, but instead of

rushing to see Kendell, she started down the street toward Muffin Top. The two met a few houses from Scratch and Sniff. The bandleader knelt on the brick sidewalk, hugged the hellhound, and wiped the animal's nose.

"What's that about?" Kendell asked.

Lynn returned from fetching Cupcake. "I guess you haven't seen the pups in a while. Colin must have gotten a lick in from his cane to the side of Muffin Top's head. From the way she acted during your ordeal at the warehouse, nothing seems broken, but there's a scar on her jaw that will probably be a lifelong reminder of her adventure in hell."

Kendell began reconsidering letting Colin remain in his hell. Some actions were out of bounds, and hurting a dog— no matter how threatening—was number one on that list. "I'm going to kill that dog molester."

Minerva leaned out the driver's side window of her VW. "Not if Polly gets to him first. I think you may have already found Muffin Top's new mama, once Cheesecake says it's all right of course."

Lynn sat on the bottom step and kept her arm around Cupcake. "If it's not too much to ask, I'd like to look after this little love."

Myles didn't say anything, but the bond between a boy and his dog was unmistakable. The tenderness prevented Kendell from making a snarky comment at his expense. "Then it's settled. Every pup has a home. Now all we need to do is get there."

Minerva started up the grumpy VW. "All aboard for the swamp tour. Hopefully, Sanguine will have made her way back to the jetty by the time we get there."

With Colin secured in the past, the light of day surrounding her, and everyone she cared about except Sanguine safely in the bus, Kendell felt more relaxed than she had in a long time.

"Is anyone else really tired?" Lynn asked.

"And hungry?" Scraper added.

Kendell hadn't bothered analyzing her body's demands. "We moved forward in time—based on how I'm feeling, I'd guess by a couple of days. Don't give in to your body's needs. Falling asleep probably wouldn't do any good, assuming sleep is possible. We'll be headed home soon enough."

The bus swerved slightly from the edge of the road to the middle under Minerva's fatigued control. "I'll be okay so long as the old swamp witch doesn't move time along any further. Another hour or two, and I'd be a goner."

Polly straightened up in her seat. "Right. The one sure way I know of to keep us all from dying in hell is to sing."

The rest of the trip out to the bayou felt like a high school bus ride to a singing competition.

When Minerva turned onto the gravel parking lot on the jetty that bordered the swamp, everyone was exhausted. Even the VW sounded like it wanted to go to sleep. "At least Sanguine made it out okay, but from the way she's slumped over in the canoe, I'm guessing she succumbed to the need for sleep."

Kendell's body ached as she pulled at the open door to get out of the bus. "Wait here. I'll go get her."

She almost hated waking Sanguine. Sleep had eluded everyone for so long that the image of the girl with her eyes closed almost made Kendell weep. *Fuck this. The only time I'm this emotional is when I'm exhausted.*

She used self-incriminating anger to help her shake Sanguine, but the woman didn't wake. "Myles, come help. She's not coming out of it."

He hurried to her side. "What's wrong with her?"

She didn't want the rest of the group to hear. "Remember how we couldn't sleep while we were chasing Colin? That tired-but-awake state wasn't one we could change. I'm afraid the same might be true if any of us falls asleep now."

"She's in a coma?"

Kendell wasn't sure what to think. The person with the most information about this reality was currently not in a position to talk. "I don't know. We need to get her into the bus and back to Baron Samedi. Maybe he can help."

"And if he can't?"

Thinking while dazed from lack of sleep made Kendell's head hurt. "Then we carry her back to our reality and hope she snaps out of it."

Myles lifted the comatose woman into his arms and followed Kendell back to the van.

"She's okay, just knocked out. We can't afford for any of us to join her in dreamland, though, so let's keep singing. Do whatever you can to stay awake."

Kendell didn't have trouble staying awake for the ride back to the city. Sanguine, nestled between her and Myles, was enough of a warning of what would happen should she give in to her desire for sleep.

Even with the road noise, the engine screaming under

their bench seat, and the rocking of the van, Kendell continually tried to wake Sleeping Beauty. "Come on, Sanguine. Don't do this to me. I need you."

But no amount of shaking or enticing could wake the woman on the half hour drive back to the bank.

∾

MYLES WASN'T comfortable leaving Sanguine in the bus all on her own in such a vulnerable state. Logic argued that Colin was not around, but he'd proven too wily to discount. Baron Samedi, however, would need everyone's help to escape back to Guinee. Before following Kendell out of the bus, Myles shoved Doughnut Hole next to the sleeping woman. "Keep an eye on her for me, okay?"

The hellhound slumped against the woman as if he too would like to catch a nap.

"No falling asleep. You've got a job to do. I won't be long."

Up in the office, Baron Samedi was as pale as the white bones that were painted on every exposed section of his skin. Time seemed to be doing a double whammy on the voodoo loa, who occupied too many dimensions at the same time. "The gates are secure."

"And now it's time we got you back to Guinee. What do you need us to do?"

The man's long coat hung loosely on his emaciated shoulders. "The gates to Guinee must be opened. I couldn't risk it while the gates to life were being constructed, but there's a catch."

Myles well understood what was involved in moving from one realm to the next. "They have to be opened in order, but without time existing in this dimension, it wouldn't be possible for those in Guinee to see the difference."

"Exactly." He turned toward the elegant bookcase behind the desk. "Though I am the seventh voodoo loa, I can't open my gate from this side. It will be up to me to make the final offering. Papa Ghede stands watch in my absence. For me to pass through to Guinee, the other gates will have to be opened simultaneously. Maybe if Papa Ghede sees all the offerings at once, he'll understand my dilemma and let me pass."

Kendell had been the one to make the offerings at the gates while Myles had been a prisoner of Baron Malveaux in the afterlife. "There are six of us left conscious. If we each take a gate, can you set off a beacon to let us know when to make the offerings?"

He twirled his cane like a baton. "I can manage that."

Kendell wasn't finished. "Is there anything you can do for Sanguine? She fell asleep."

Samedi looked around the room, but Myles suspected he was really seeing the mirrors into other realities. "Sleeping without time is dangerous. For me to try to wake her would be worse. She could wake up at any point in her future. The young woman you know might turn into an old woman before your eyes."

"And if we leave her asleep but take her home?"

He continued to turn his cane as he thought. "She might lose some time on the rest of you. As it would likely be less than a day that she'd be asleep in this dimension, it wouldn't be physically noticeable, but it could give her a glimpse into the future. She'd experience a continuous feeling of déjà vu. The state is called déjà vecu, and it can be very disorienting."

Kendell turned to Myles. "I guess we'll have to start listening to her more closely."

"That is, if she wakes up at all," Baron Samedi continued. "Falling asleep requires a time reference for the body to know when to wake. Have you ever gotten up minutes before the alarm goes off?"

Myles didn't like where Baron Samedi was heading. "Of course."

"That's the result of your internal clock."

Kendell took Myles's hand. "But we can still wake her, right?"

Baron Samedi talked as if he were giving a lecture instead of referring to someone who'd helped free him from hell. "People wake themselves up. A person might hear something external to their dreams that reminds them about the time, but it's still the dreamer who decides to come back to consciousness."

Myles knew when a conversation was no longer progressing. "Let's get you out of here, then we can make our way back to life and deal with Sanguine. One problem at a time."

Back out in the VW, Myles felt like a bartender on a party bus as he handed out small bottles of rum, absconded from the speakeasy, to the women. "No drinking. This is strictly for the offering to the other loas of the dead.

Without time, who knows how they would interpret others partaking of their libations."

He'd seen each of the cemeteries used as the gates of Guinee but only from the inside. Kendell sat up front, doing her best to navigate with Cheesecake taking up most of the windshield. "Saint Louis No. 1 first. As there won't be a specific order, it doesn't matter who takes which station. Just be ready to pour the rum when you see the signal."

Polly was the first one out of the bus. Muffin Top jumped out after her. "We'll take this one. I've always wanted to see Marie Laveau's tomb. You don't suppose she might stop by?"

"I doubt it," Kendell said. "But if you run into trouble, send Muffin Top to Saint Louis No. 2."

Lynn rubbed Cupcake's black-and-white mane. "I'll take that cemetery. The sister dogs should be able to find each other easily enough."

Once Scraper was dropped off, it was down to Kendell and Myles riding with Minerva. Myles put his hand on the back of the driver's seat. "This is your stop. Kendell and I can walk to our locations. No matter what you see or hear, don't do anything until you see the signal and pour your libation. After that, if one of us does end up in trouble, round up who you can and head over."

"What about her?" Minerva motioned toward Sanguine, who was fast asleep on the back bench.

"If Prince Charming comes along and tries to kiss her, hit your bus horn," Myles said. "Otherwise, I think she'll be okay."

He walked Kendell to the next cemetery. With so many

hidden away in dark sections of the city, it was as if the dead really were still a part of the living. She held him close at the iron gate. "You don't need to take the sixth gate. We could switch."

Baron Kriminel wasn't exactly Myles's enemy, but his chicanery in Guinee had landed Baron Samedi's cane in Archibald Malveaux's hands during the city's first official Mardi Gras parade.

"I can handle Kriminel. He has an obligation to watch over the sixth gate. Unlike Baron Malveaux, the loa has honor. As long as the libation is offered correctly, he won't have a reason to deny Baron Samedi passage back to Guinee."

"Maybe not, but his association with Baron Malveaux bothers me. I know Colin is back in time, so opening the gates won't do him any good, but being a little cautious wouldn't be a bad idea."

Myles reached down and scratched Doughnut Hole's ear. "I'll have my guardian. He's got a sixth sense for knowing where Colin is and what he's up to."

Kendell pulled on the latch of the heavy wrought-iron gate. "Cheesecake will keep her ears peeled for Doughnut Hole's bark."

Myles waited until Kendell and her dog had turned a corner and were lost from sight among the crypts before heading down the street with his pup. Being alone in a city usually teaming with life still didn't feel natural. At least at dusk people were often eating or resting up for the night's adventures, but during the day, the lack of people was downright eerie.

"Come on, boy. Let's get a little jog in. Baron Samedi must be getting a little antsy to set off that cane."

The exercise managed to distract him from the lurking fear of who might be waiting at his destination. He could put on a brave front for Kendell, but facing Baron Kriminel did make Myles queasy. He slowed down to a stroll when he entered the city of the dead. The mausoleum he sought looked much like all the others that lined the walking path, but having seen it from the inside, Myles would never forget its marble front.

He pulled out the bottle of rum and shot glass. If everything went according to plan, he might not even have to face Baron Kriminel. He hoped none of the women would have to face their loas. Only Kendell had any experience with the guardians to Guinee.

Okay, Baron Samedi. Let's get this over with.

A green flare shot high into the sky above the French Quarter. Myles set the shot glass on the small ledge meant to hold a bouquet of flowers and poured the rum just as the ball of light exploded into seven spiraling spokes of sparks.

Baron Kriminel strolled out of the tomb as if he'd been expecting to be summoned. "You come asking another favor?"

"You know why I'm here. I suspect you're the reason I'm here."

The loa of the dead leaned against the granite side of the crypt. "Are you accusing me of trapping Baron Samedi in this witch's hell?"

"At one time, you used Baron Archibald Malveaux to

displace Baron Samedi as the seventh guardian, and now I suspect you're helping Colin Malveaux."

The dark spirit looked around the deserted grounds. "If that were true, why would I wish Baron Samedi to remain as guardian over my servant?"

"Perhaps so you can control Guinee? With him out of the way and Papa Ghede watching over his gate, you might think the time was right for a change."

"If I let him back, there might be a war."

Myles wished the rulers of Guinee would learn how to look after themselves without pulling in the living. "Better an isolated war than one spread across dimensions. Baron Samedi won't survive long in this hell."

"His passing would create an unstable boundary between the living, the dead, and the *deep waters*. If war does happen in Guinee, though, you might get sucked into the conflict."

Myles hadn't expected anything different.

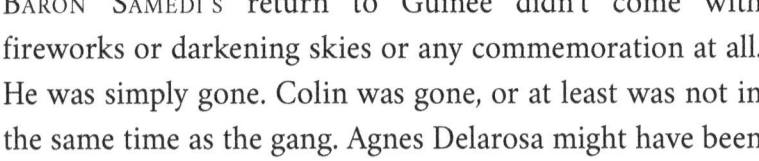

Baron Samedi's return to Guinee didn't come with fireworks or darkening skies or any commemoration at all. He was simply gone. Colin was gone, or at least was not in the same time as the gang. Agnes Delarosa might have been around somewhere, but with her granddaughter in a coma, she wasn't reachable.

Their task mostly complete, and with no one watching, Myles and Doughnut Hole danced down the neutral ground of Canal Street like a one-man, one-dog second line. "One last task, boy, and we'll be home."

Kendell and Cheesecake were the first to join in on the miniature parade. "I've always wanted to dance down the middle of Canal. Now all we need is a little music."

The rhythmic honking of the battered horn on Minerva's VW announced that accompaniment was on the way. As the van reached the back of the growing parade, Polly—with tambourine in hand—jumped out of the slow-moving vehicle to join in the dance. With Cupcake and Muffin Top following the bandleader, there were more dogs in the procession than human companions.

Scraper on electric bass and Lynn on mobile keyboard made their music heard through the open windows of the van. Minerva continued to keep time with the bus's horn.

Polly spun between Myles and Kendell. "We figured out how to power the instruments from the old VW. That thing is amazingly versatile. With the modifications from Delphine and Professor Yates, we could amp up this whole town."

Minerva took up the opening rhythm to "Iko Iko," adding in flashing headlights for emphasis. The traditional New Orleans parade song quickly had everyone singing along, even Myles, though he had more confidence in his dance moves than his off-key singing.

Cheesecake took lead of the second line, howling out her interpretation of the song. With dog, human, dog, human, the interspersed multispecies line of revelers weaved across the streetcar tracks, the bus following along behind.

For a moment, Myles forgot he was dancing in hell, and

in that moment, he sensed someone not of the troop dancing next to him. "Charlie, what are you doing here?"

His fellow bartender's presence made about as much sense as a dead person showing up in a dream. "I heard there was a second line. You know I've never been able to resist a good party."

Even Myles didn't know when or where the trip out of hell was going to take place. "How did you hear about it?"

"How does anyone hear about any great gig in New Orleans? Word of mouth!"

Myles still wasn't sure he believed what he was seeing. His exhaustion had a way of making reality a little hazy. If it was really Charlie, then Myles couldn't think of a more welcome addition.

His friend pointed beyond Kendell, who was dancing in front of Doughnut Hole. A multicolored piece of fabric was floating on a breeze, but as Myles focused on it, Delphine de Galpion filled out the garment. Her dance moves put everyone else's to shame.

It's working. He wanted to shout to Kendell to sing louder. As she spun around, he noticed she had her eyes closed. He feared distracting her might break the spell. *Good girl. Keep going.* Maybe she'd hear his thought, or maybe not, but either way, he knew he was witnessing her powers in action.

The long-limbed, gangly body of Professor Yates joined in next to Polly. He kept far enough from the lead singer to avoid hitting her with his exuberant dance moves.

Myles turned back to face the front of the procession. Tears filled his eyes at the thought of his friends joining in on the second line out of hell. Up ahead, like a military escort, Police Lieutenant Joe Cazenave and his paramilitary troop marched in formation. Myles sighed with relief at seeing his friend wearing his police uniform. Joe had returned to the force. Whatever danger had sent the cops to Myles's old apartment must have been cleared up. *Life must have continued on without us.* He wondered how much time had passed while they'd been caught in the no-time of hell.

A streetcar bell joined in with the VW bus's horn. The number of people around the procession grew exponentially. People Myles recognized were joined by others—friends of friends—until the main street that cut through New Orleans was as full as a Mardi Gras celebration.

Through it all, Kendell kept her eyes closed as she sang and danced as if she were alone.

When the fifty-pound hellhound in front of Myles reverted to a two-pound puppy of uncoordinated black fur, he knew they were home.

———

*M*yles found it oddly calming to be back at the bar, serving drinks beside Charlie. The musicians onstage played cheesy '80s covers without calling forth magic. Drunk tourists danced badly and hit on each other to avoid spending the night alone. No one in the club, with the exception of Charlie, knew about the parallel realities or the hell Myles had helped secure.

Though returning to a normal life reduced the burden of standing watch over the devil, after a week of the usual routine, Myles lost interest in the predictable banter that buzzed in his ears every night like a swarm of mosquitos. "Charlie, I'm going to knock off early tonight."

"Headed back to the Scratchy Dog?" Charlie always could see right through Myles.

"I thought I'd walk Kendell to her gig. The girls are playing a late-night set." Myles felt a comfort with his fellow travelers to hell that was hard to put into words.

The head bartender cleaned a beer stein with slow deliberation. "I get it. After a month in dimensional isolation, crowds must induce a little claustrophobia for you. We've got enough staff. Do what you need to do."

From Charlie's tone, Myles could tell that he was feeling a little on the outs as a friend. "Come with me. Be a little irresponsible for once."

The jab brought forth a laugh from the boisterous manager. "I'm usually the one getting you into trouble." Though the bar was still hopping, Charlie took off his bar apron. "With you gone, I've been training Raven as my assistant. I suppose tonight's as good as any to see how well she manages shorthanded with no notice."

Myles hadn't meant to dump the night's work on the seasoned bartender. "So long as you think she can handle it. I'd hate to show up for my next shift to find the labels peeled off the bottles in protest." Walking the streets of the Quarter with his friend at his side helped Myles breathe a little easier. "I hope convincing you to play hooky won't get you into trouble with the boss."

"I got you the job. It only seems fair for you to get me out of mine. After a year of listening to the same musical set list every night, I'm about to pay a brass band to set up on the corner. Anything would beat another rendition of "Take Me Home Tonight.""

They climbed the stairs to his and Kendell's apartment. "Watch for the puppies. They've become escape artists. Apparently, they think all of New Orleans is their backyard."

"After what you told me about them being hellhounds, I

can't say as how I blame them."

Myles pushed the door open far enough for the three playful balls of fur to come out and bark at the stranger. "The only thing that's demonic about these guys is the way they can chew a sandal to shreds."

As with everyone who entered the apartment, Charlie was overcome with the cuteness and on the floor playing with the puppies before Myles got the door shut.

Kendell came out of the bedroom in her tank top, short black skirt, and ripped fishnet stockings—her typical band attire. "And I thought Cheesecake made a racket when someone was at the door."

With another man in the room, Myles gave Kendell a more restrained embrace than usual. "We thought we'd tag along tonight."

He knew she understood. Every member of the team had found it uncomfortable being without the others for any length of time.

"So this is Sleeping Beauty." Charlie knelt next to the couch where Sanguine lay in repose. "You don't think maybe a kiss from me might wake her?"

Had the woman not been in a coma, Kendell's laugh might well have woken her. "I love you like a brother, Charlie, but you're not the one she's waiting for."

He swiveled around on his toes. "Any idea what might bring her out of her magical sleep?"

"We hoped once we all got some rest she might come out of it, but I guess Baron Samedi was right. Her internal clock must be on the fritz."

Charlie got up before the puppies had a chance to knock

him back down to the floor. "So you're just going to leave her like this?"

"Of course not," Myles said. "I need to contact the loas of the dead."

"Those dudes again? When have they ever helped you?"

Myles had to admit, when it came to a crisis, it was Charlie and not the loas who came to the rescue. "They understand these interdimensional problems. We're a little short on expertise here. Even Madam de Galpion hasn't dealt with someone who's come back from hell while asleep. We did already try our living resources." Though he wasn't a fan of Delphine, he had first checked her library for a solution.

Kendell grabbed her guitar case. "We can talk on the way."

Cheesecake jumped onto the ottoman, taking up her usual protective spot to keep an eye on her human and puppy charges.

MYLES SNUCK out the back door of the Scratchy Dog while the band was busy setting up their equipment and Charlie flirted with the woman behind the bar.

The hidden speakeasy was right where it had been in hell. Myles tried not to make too much noise as he yanked the old pallet away from the wall and struggled with the fake shutters' latches. Kendell would be out to join him soon.

He didn't need to call forth a loa at the club—making the

rum offering at the apartment would have worked just as well—but after all he'd been through, he felt more at ease having a little separation between his life and his work.

He grabbed the bottle of rum from behind the bar and sat at the outdoor metal table. For a moment, he considered pouring only one glass. Sitting outside drinking while listening to Kendell and the band in the next room had more than a slight appeal, but he added a splash of rum to the second glass just the same.

When Papa Ghede materialized in the second chair with cane in hand, Myles thought about tossing his drink in the loa's face. "I'm not dealing with that fucking stick again. Baron Samedi took it with him when he left hell. Whatever new problem you have with that damn thing, you can just—"

Papa Ghede pointed the handle toward Myles. "It's yours."

He sat, stunned, for a moment. Marie Laveau's hand bones were still wrapped around the staff. The silver skull glowed from the green stone it encompassed. "What are you talking about?"

The head loa waved the end of the cane at him. "Baron Samedi needed it to help establish the gates of hell. His powers don't come from this stick, though. If someone holds onto a possession long enough, that thing is bound to pick up on the individual's energy. You of all people must know that."

"Okay, but why are you giving it to me? We worked really hard getting that thing *out* of the land of the living."

He laid the cane on the table. "You prevented Colin

Malveaux from acquiring it, but this cane was always meant to find its way to you."

"But how is that possible? The history of this thing goes back way before I was born."

Papa Ghede downed the rum with one swallow. "Do I really need to explain time to you *again?*"

Myles refilled the loa's glass, less out of respect than as an apology for not seeing the obvious. "After my firsthand experience in hell, I suppose not."

"Take the cane, and see for yourself."

Myles was actually afraid to touch it. "What happens if I accept it?"

"You won't have omnipotent powers if that's what's worrying you. Consider the cane another marker on your life journey."

A marker to where? The loas never did anything without a self-serving reason. "What's in it for you?"

Papa Ghede rolled the cane from side to side across the table. "Colin Malveaux is secure—for now. Baron Samedi sealed the access from Colin's hell to Guinee, so we have no way to keep an eye on his shenanigans. You and your friends, however, have established the connections we usually enjoy. By having the cane, you can be our emissary should the unfortunate happen."

"You mean should Colin escape."

Kendell put her hand on Myles's shoulder before he knew she'd joined them. "What would happen if Colin did find a way out of hell?"

"He would be a devil among the living. The powers he's learned in his imprisonment could transfer into life. My hope is that Myles will learn to use the powers of the cane before that happens."

Myles didn't like being used so blatantly. "You don't give our hell much of a chance, do you?"

"In my experience with devils, it's best to have contingency plans. Plus, Colin isn't the only threat out there. You two need to be ready."

Kendell clamped her fingers hard onto Myles's shoulder. "What do you expect of me?"

"From our side, the cane will obey Myles, but he isn't the one who secured its use among the living. Since you spun the silver skull back in place while in hell, when Myles takes the cane, you will replace Marie Laveau as the guardian."

Myles could see there was no way of rejecting the gift. Before Kendell could argue him out of his course of action, he reached over and grabbed the stick. Once he stood the black rod upright, the hand bones fell to the ground and turned to dust.

Papa Ghede's continuous smile spread so far across his face that his eyes squeezed shut. "You won't regret your choice."

Myles couldn't let the assumption go unchallenged. "I didn't have a choice."

The dark loa reached into his dusty, long coat and turned to Kendell. "I have something for you too. Consider it a replacement for the golden pick."

"Whatever you have, I don't want it. The golden pick proved to me that I have all the magic I'll ever need already inside me."

He pulled out an envelope and placed it on the table.

"My offer isn't of the paranormal variety. Of the gates of hell that you established, this building is the only one that isn't physically secure. Mary's plantation on the other side of the river has been in her family for generations. Miss Fleur will always be welcome in the convent, which, as part of the Catholic Church will never be torn down. The bank—"

"I get it," Kendell said. "Of all the places we used, this is the only one we don't have control over."

He slid the envelope over to her. "With this deed, now you do. Both the stage that works for the band's gate and this courtyard bar that Myles guards are covered by this paperwork."

She pulled out the yellowed paper. "How did you end up with it? Don't tell me it's some poor soul's attempt at buying their freedom."

"Nothing so nefarious. Haven't you ever wondered why these buildings so seldom come on the market? Those of us in the afterlife control most of the buildings along Frenchmen Street and the Quarter in some fashion."

She gave him the squinting stare of suspicion Myles had seen too many times. "If you own the property, why give it to me?"

"Voodoo versus Wicca. Even though you are a voodoo priestess, you aren't of the afterlife. The spirit of Agnes Delarosa will rest more easily knowing the property is in your hands. Were I to keep it, a conflict might arise."

Myles had enough to worry about without adding the prospect of an interparanormal war. "So she'd own this place free and clear? No future payback or expectations?"

"As long as the two gates from the living to hell exist in this place, she'll be unable to sell it. Should Colin find a way out, or should he be dealt with some other way, Kendell can dispose of the property as she sees fit. From our side, the deal fulfills our debt to her."

"What debt?" Kendell asked.

Papa Ghede stood up. "Time prevents me from going into details."

Myles suspected the time in question didn't have to do with Papa Ghede rushing off. "You're referring to something Kendell does in the future?"

"It's not for me to dictate your paths, only to add a little encouragement where I can."

Kendell hurried out her questions. "What about Sanguine? How do we wake her?"

"Sanguine Delarosa is not part of the voodoo continuum. She fell asleep in a realm created by her grandmother. All I can tell you is the fundamental truth that people move toward what they love. Find a way to attract her attention to something about life that gives her passion, and you might be able to wake her."

～

KENDELL WOULD HAVE HAPPILY SAT on the floor, playing with the puppies all day, every day. "Why couldn't they have given me a lifetime supply of puppies? Why did it have to be a drafty old nightclub?"

Polly had just finished her shift watching the pups at the apartment. When it came to Muffin Top, Polly was as infatuated as Kendell had been with Cheesecake as a puppy. "At least the band doesn't have to worry about finding gigs. Admit it—owning property, especially if there's no mortgage, isn't all bad."

"I've just never seen myself as a businesswoman."

The bandleader lay flat on the floor so that she was eye to eye—or eye to tongue—with the dogs. "Charlie said he'd manage the club and tend bar with Myles. You know the girls and I will help secure other bands. And we've all been sworn to secrecy, so you won't be thought of as some rich, snooty wannabe bohemian. Your reputation's safe. So what have you got to worry about?"

Kendell knew her friend was right, just as she knew Papa Ghede was only trying to secure what they'd all created. "I know. Don't for a minute think I'm taking the help for granted. I'd freak out if it weren't for all you guys. Why do I feel so trapped?"

Polly finally sat up, taking Muffin Top into her lap. "I believe the word you're trying to avoid is *responsibility*. I get it. When we first got the gig at the Scratchy Dog, I was thrilled. The feeling lasted for about five minutes. After that, the reality of showing up on time, making sure we packed the room, and praying for enough tips to keep all you girls in po'boys and beer settled in. You'll get used to that knot in your stomach just like I have."

"Thanks a lot. I haven't eaten a full meal in two days."

"What does Myles have to say?"

Kendell leaned back against the ottoman so Cheesecake could snuggle her head. The mother dog needed her love. "He says it'll be good for both of us. He and Charlie are over there now, making plans. I still think his name should go on the deed with mine, but he's being stubborn."

"You'll wear him down. I've never known you not to get your way with him. What about that cane?" Polly's tone was a little too measured for the question to have been spontaneous.

"He fears it like I fear the club. But he's doing his best to figure out what powers might be inside it. Did you hear the fireworks last night?"

"Sure. I figured there was another convention in town."

Doughnut Hole was pulling on Kendell's sandal for attention. "Nope. That was Myles. I made him sleep out on the veranda with Doughnut Hole."

For the first time, Polly looked more interested in the conversation than in Muffin Top. "That was Myles? What did he do to get banished, and why would you make poor little Doughnut Hole sleep in the cold?"

New Orleans in early fall is hardly cold, even at night. "He'd been stroking that stick like it was Aladdin's lamp. All he managed to do was make that green stone under the skull glow, so I teased him, saying it looked like he was trying to jerk it off."

Polly wasn't doing a very good job at suppressing her laugh. "And what did he say?"

"He looked me straight in the eye and said, 'That's right, baby. Glowing green voodoo jizz.' That's when I told him he wasn't sharing my bed."

"And Doughnut Hole?"

Kendell scratched Cheesecake's head. "He's getting a

little rambunctious with his sisters. We're going to need to wean them soon. Why are guys so gross sometimes?"

Polly lifted Muffin Top to her face. "This one's coming with me, right?"

Kendell felt Cheesecake go rigid under her touch. "Soon. Mama dog's not quite ready to let go of her brood."

Polly reached over and petted Doughnut Hole's curly hair. "You didn't really make them sleep outside all night, did you?"

Kendell doubted there was anything Myles could do to make her that angry. "No. After an hour in bed alone I went out and cuddled with Myles. We both love sleeping outside, so it wasn't really a banishment."

SANGUINE STOOD on the wooden dock over Lake Pontchartrain. Wind from the hurricane over the horizon sent waves that lapped against the piers and ruffled the snow-white feathers of her shoulder-to-heel-length wings. Her backless ivory dress covered her body from her neck to the tops of her golden sandals. The breeze exhilarated her as if she were already airborne. With a half dozen running strides, she was at the edge of the pier. She launched off the last board while spreading her ten-foot wingspan. Instantly, she was gliding over the water. She folded her arms against her chest and moved her wings against the night air. The massive appendages quickly had her well clear of the lake.

Dream stages had been her passion as a novice witch learning from her grandmother. Though such stages were typically only useful for accessing the subconscious, in this dimension that straddled the real and the make-believe, she could spread her wings literally as well as figuratively. Dear, sweet Kendell would watch over her body for as long as Sanguine needed to complete her mission.

She reached for the hilt of the sword that hung from the sash of her dress and drew it forth like an avenging angel. Her wings beat hard against the wind. Her hair and dress rippled with savage fury.

Alone with her adversary in hell, she had her plan firmly in mind. Her grandmother, wise as she was, had been wrong. Kendell had been wrong. The adventure to hell with the gang acting like some Saturday-morning cartoon had accomplished only one thing—it had left Sanguine with the freedom to act on her own.

First, I'm going to kill you. She didn't know what would happen if Colin left this hell, but anything would be better than him having access to the gates back to the living. *Why do you people keep underestimating him? Where there's a door, there's multiple ways of opening it.*

She wasn't about to give him the opportunity to figure out how to subvert the idiotic seven gates. Sending Colin into some other realm, however, was just the first step.

Throughout her Wiccan training, Sanguine had been taught about the fluid nature of time. However, until she'd seen firsthand how the mystical energy could be made to stand still or even turned backward, she'd never grasped the importance of her grandmother's lessons. *I get it now, old witch. You built the playing field and set the rules, but you couldn't engage in the game. You needed me to be your advocate. Once I untether him from this end point of his reality, I'll go back and prevent Archibald Malveaux's evil from ever taking root among the living.*

BOOK LIST

ABOUT THE AUTHOR

G.A. Chase is the pen name for Greg Chase. He is a science fiction and paranormal author living in New Orleans with his wife, fellow author Deanna Chase, and their two shih tzu dogs. On any given day you can find him behind his computer, people watching in the quarter, or out in his studio creating stories in glass. His glass work can be found at www.chase-designs.com.

www.gregchaseauthor.com